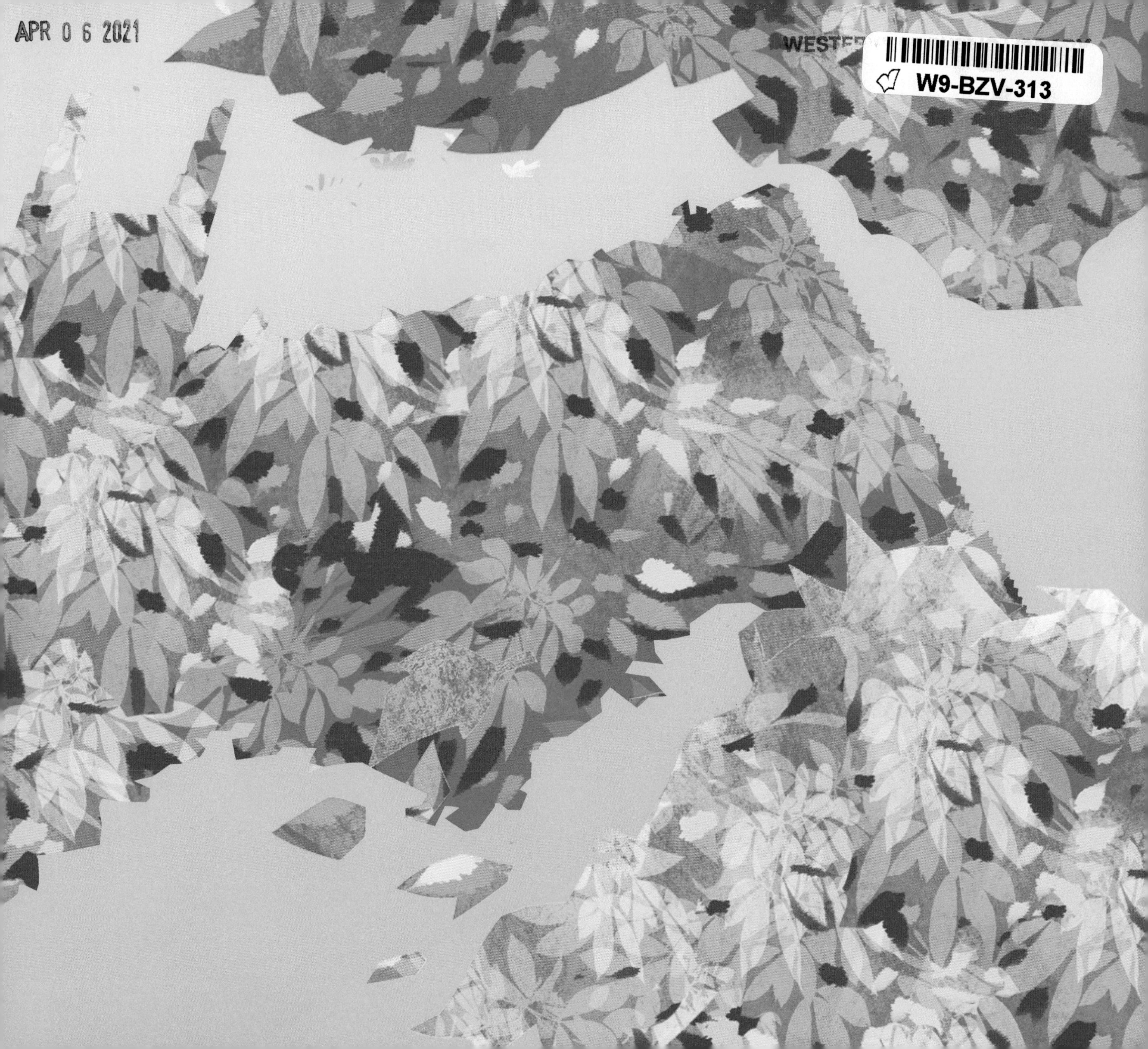

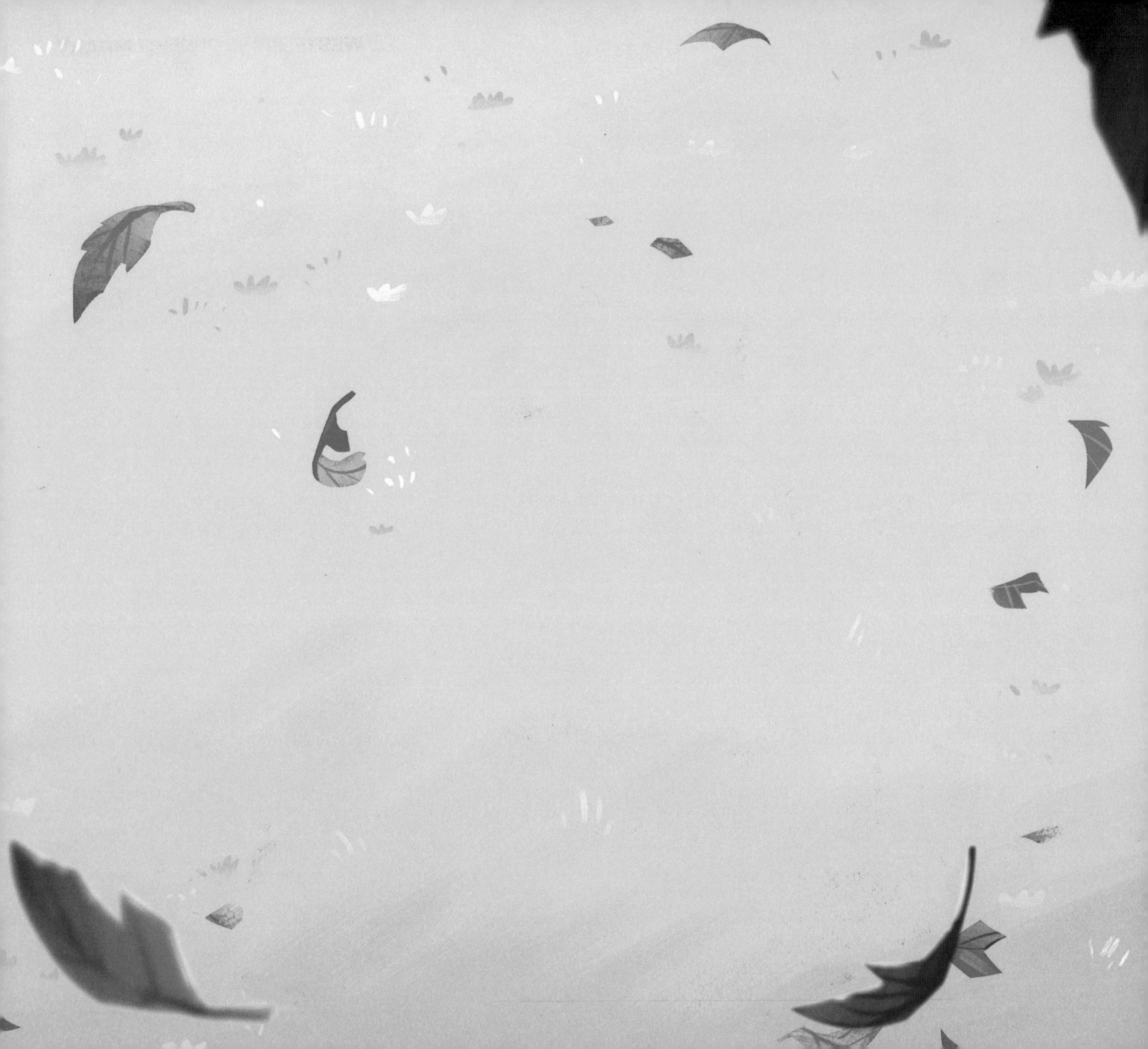

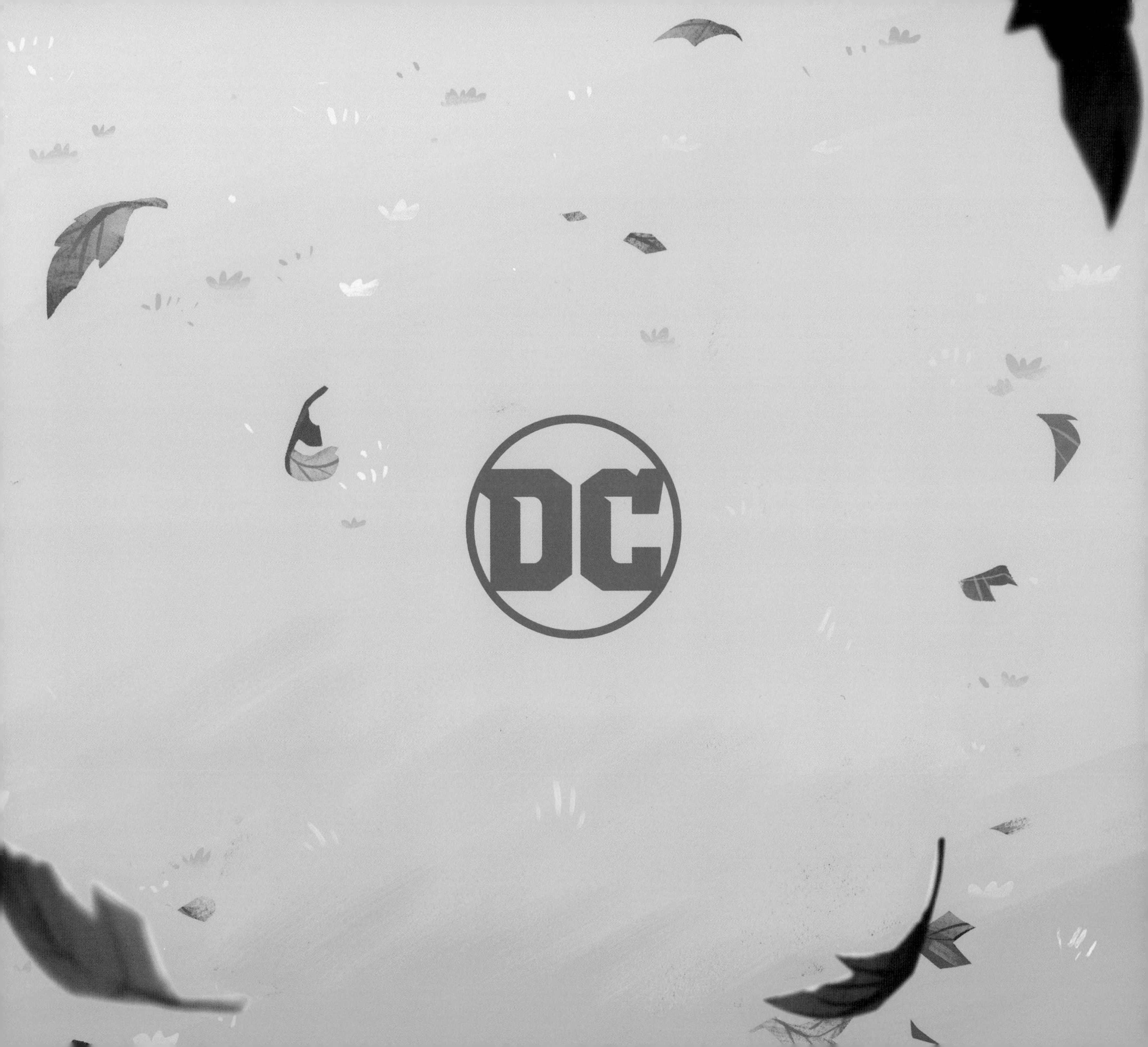
DC

DC Super Heroes are published by Capstone Editions, an imprint of Capstone.
1710 Roe Crest Drive
North Mankato, Minnesota 56003
www.capstonepub.com

Library of Congress Cataloging-in-Publication Data
Names: Dahl, Michael, author. I Lozano, Omar, illustrator.
Title: Batman and Batgirl unite! : a book about teamwork / by Michael Dahl;
    illustrated by Omar Lozano.
Description: North Mankato, Minnesota: Capstone Editions, an imprint of
    Capstone, [2021] I Series: DC super heroes I "Batman created by Bob Kane
    with Bill Finger." I Audience: Ages 5-7. I Audience: Grades K-1. I Summary:
    "Batman and Batgirl are two of the World's Greatest Super Heroes. They
    have the brains, tools, and talent to take down Gotham City's most
    dangerous bad guys. But what's their most powerful skill of all? Teamwork!"–
    Provided by publisher.
Identifiers: LCCN 2020031418 (print) I LCCN 2020031419 (ebook) I
    ISBN 9781684462841 (hardcover) I ISBN 9781684463534 (pdf) I ISBN
    9781684463633 (kindle edition)
Subjects: LCSH: Graphic novels. I CYAC: Graphic novels. I Superheroes–Fiction.
Classification: LCC PZ7.7.D34 Bat 2021 (print) I LCC PZ7.7.D34 (ebook) I DDC
    741.5/973–dc23
LC record available at https://lccn.loc.gov/2020031418
LC ebook record available at https://lccn.loc.gov/2020031419

Designer: Brann Garvey

Printed and bound in the United States of America.   PO3837

BATMAN AND BATGIRL UNITE!

A BOOK ABOUT TEAMWORK

by Michael Dahl

illustrated by Omar Lozano

BATMAN CREATED BY
Bob Kane with Bill Finger

CAPSTONE EDITIONS
a Capstone imprint

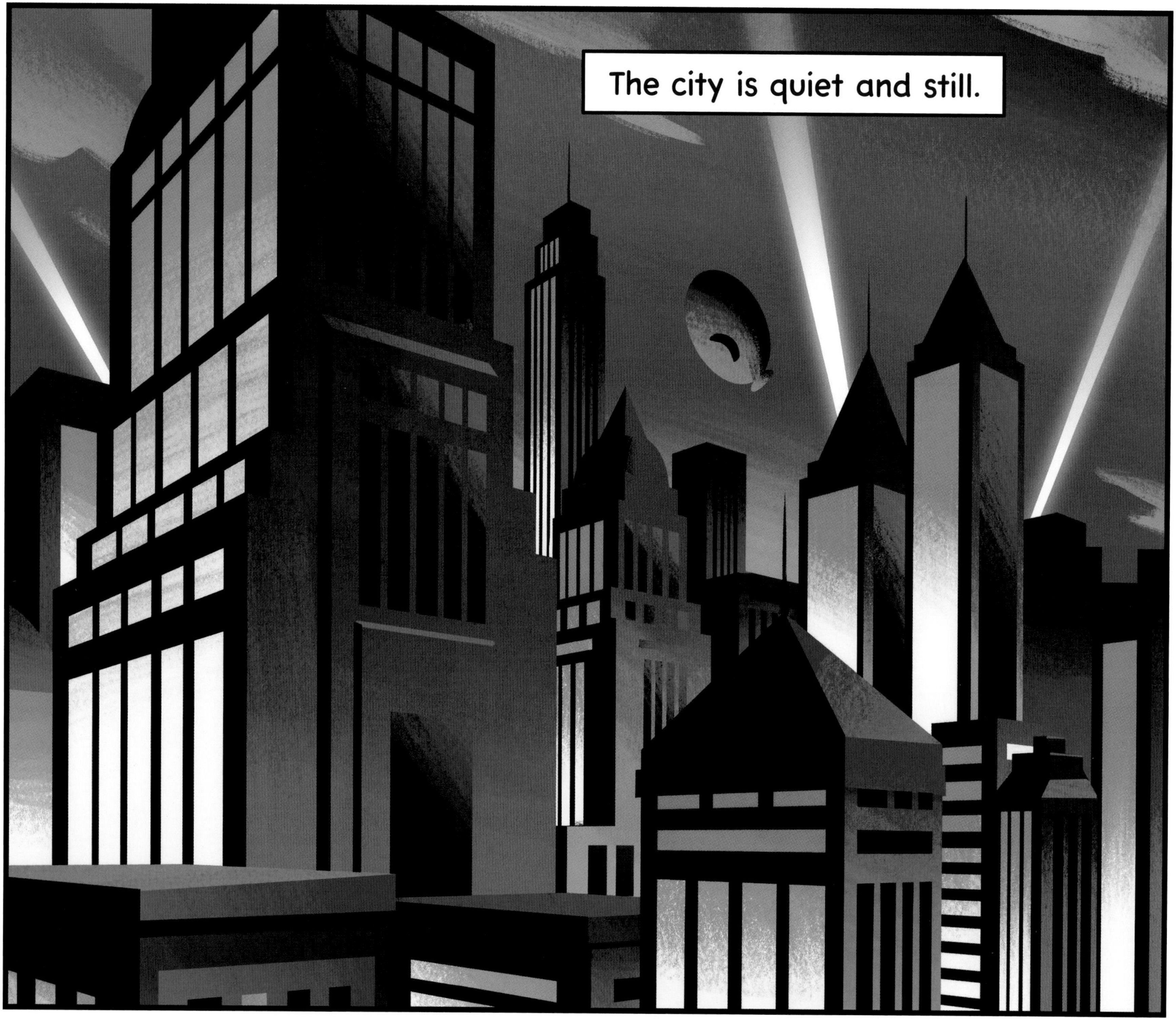
The city is quiet and still.

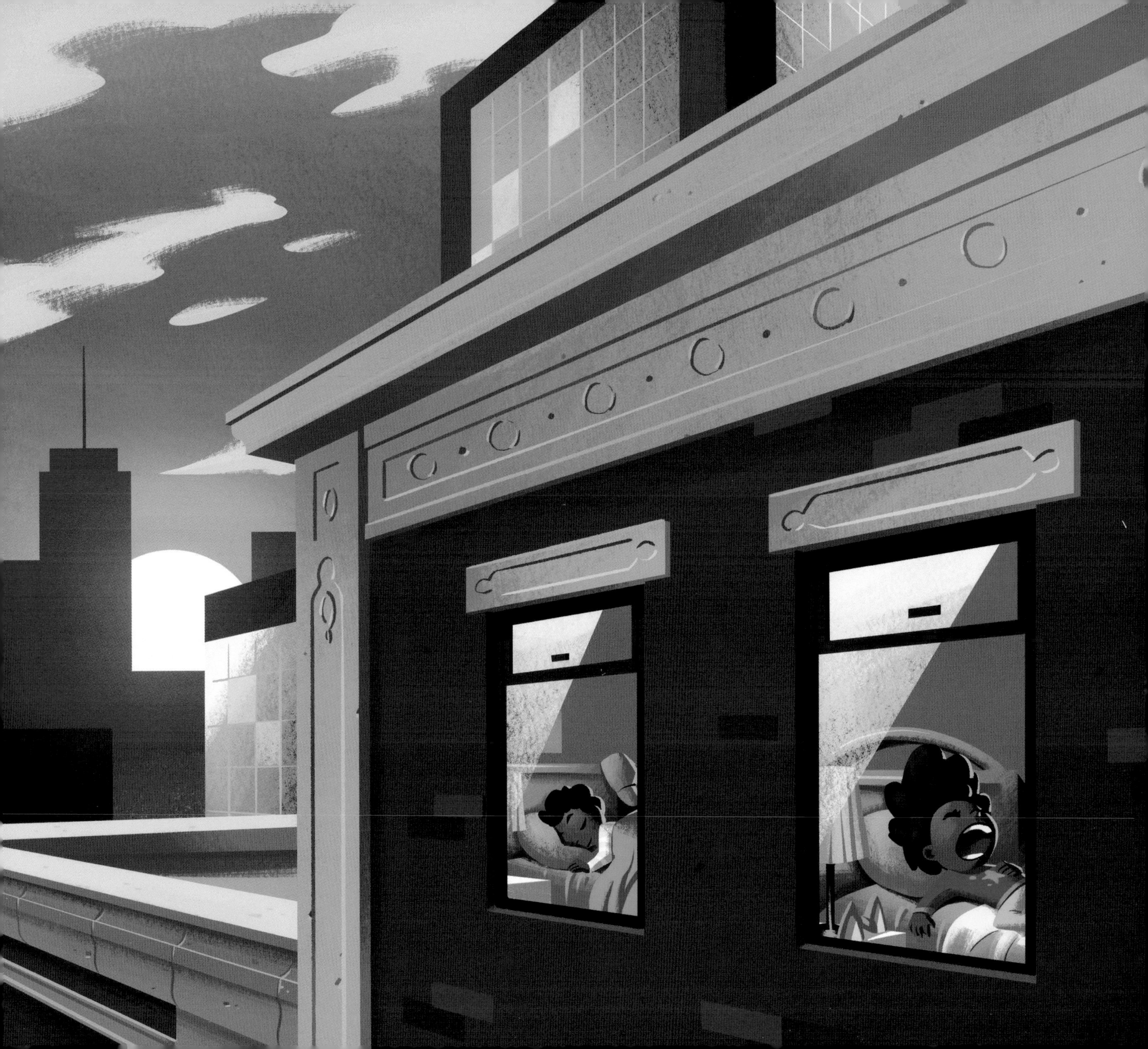

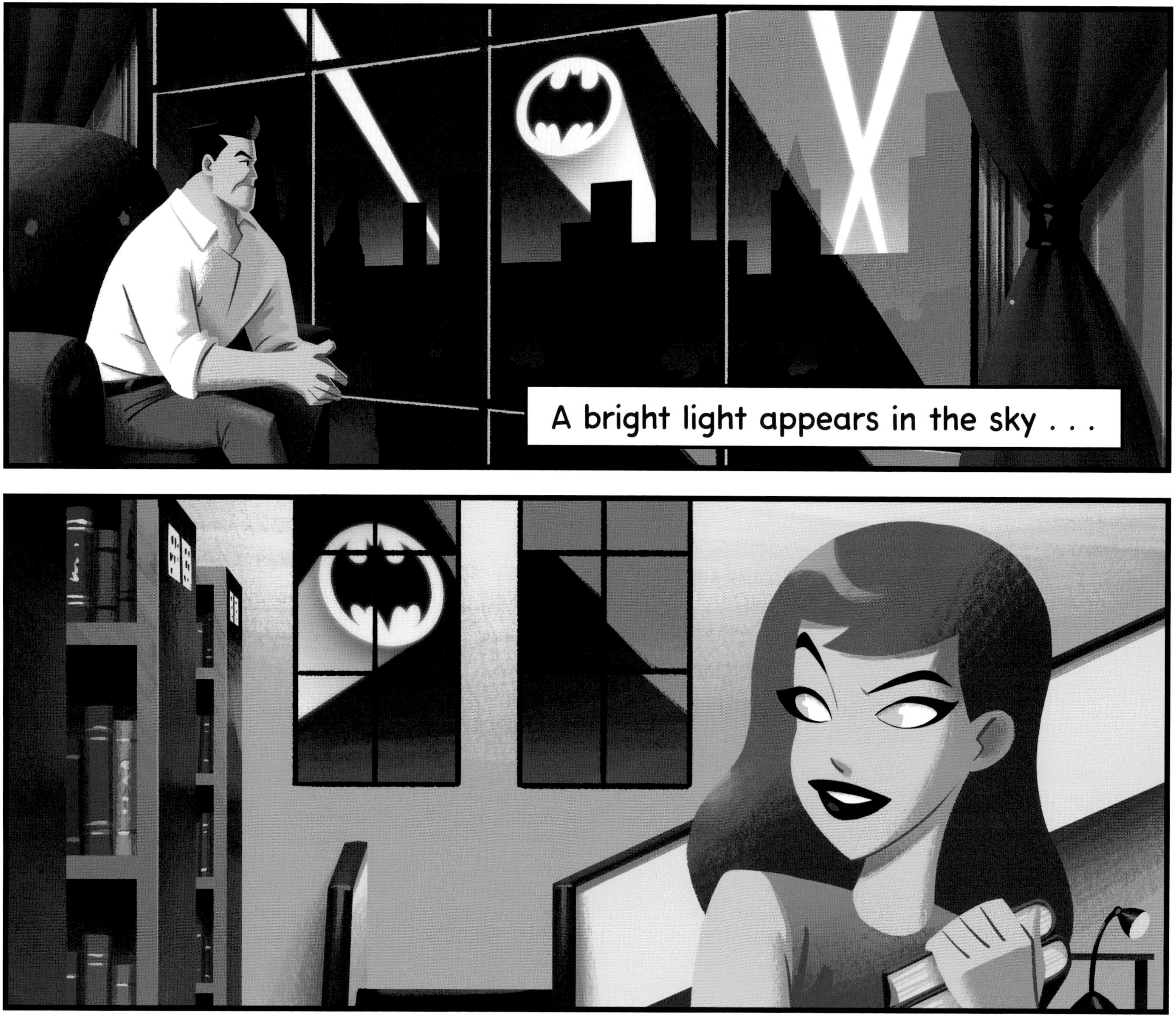
A bright light appears in the sky . . .

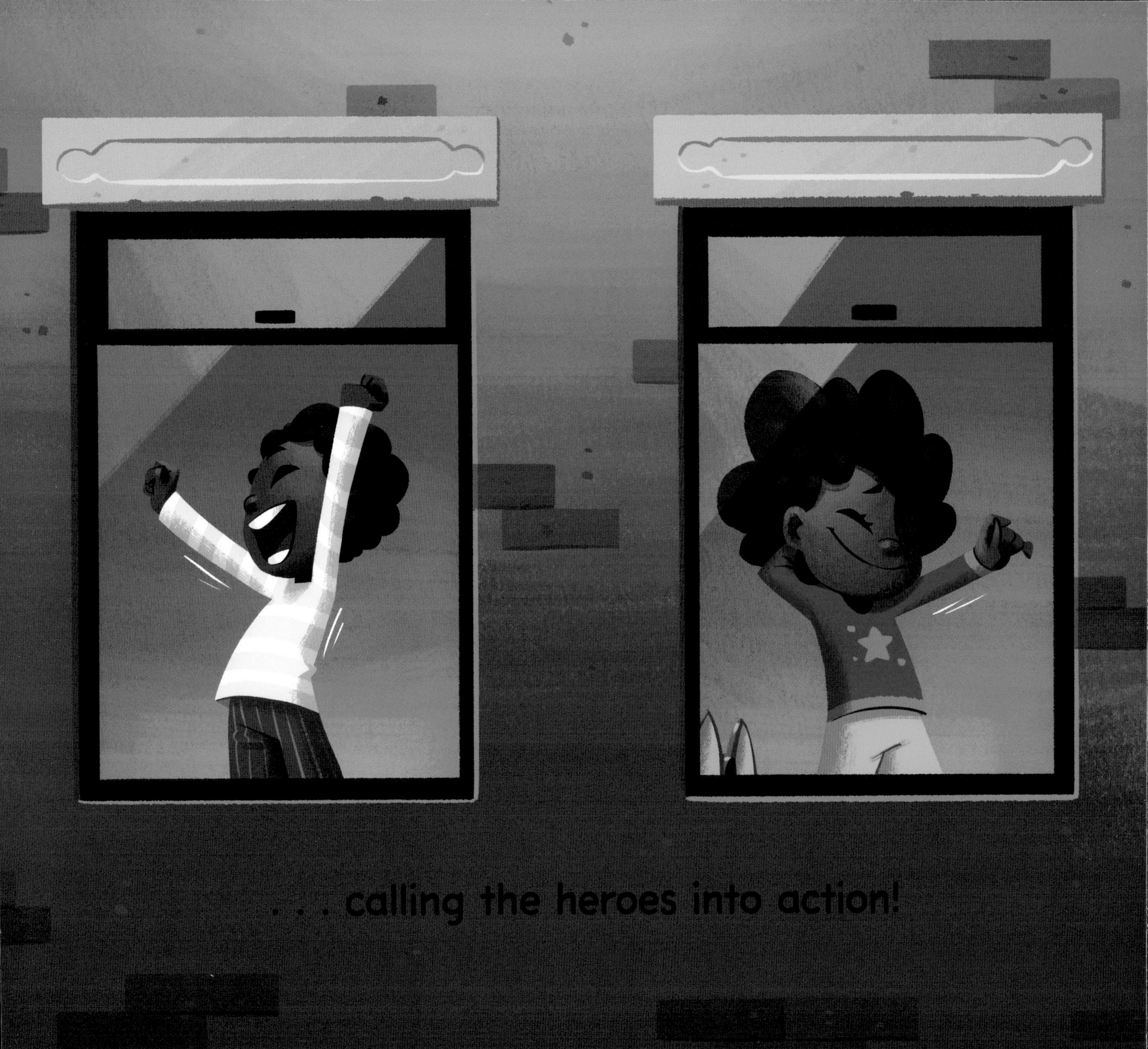

. . . calling the heroes into action!

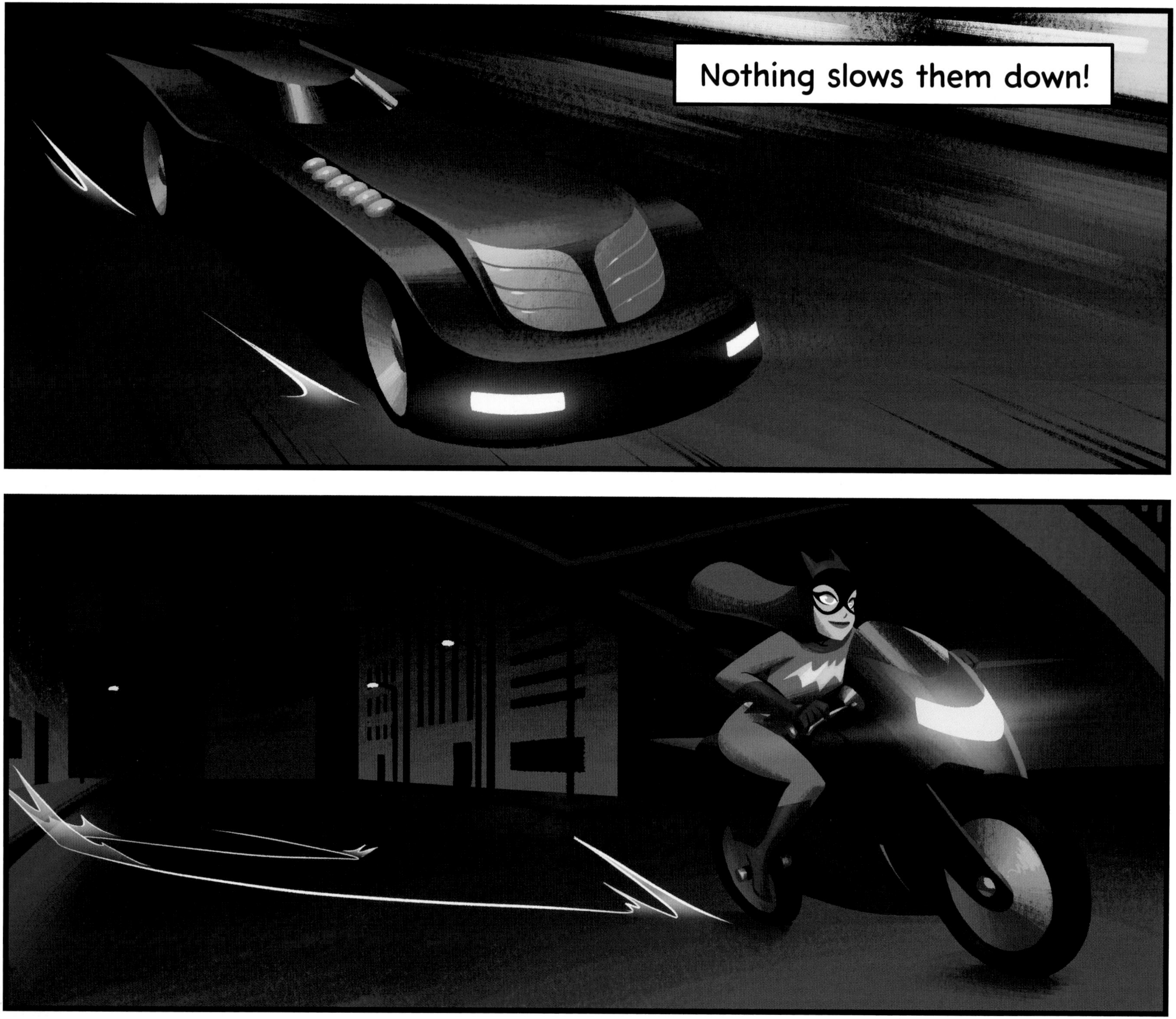
Nothing slows them down!

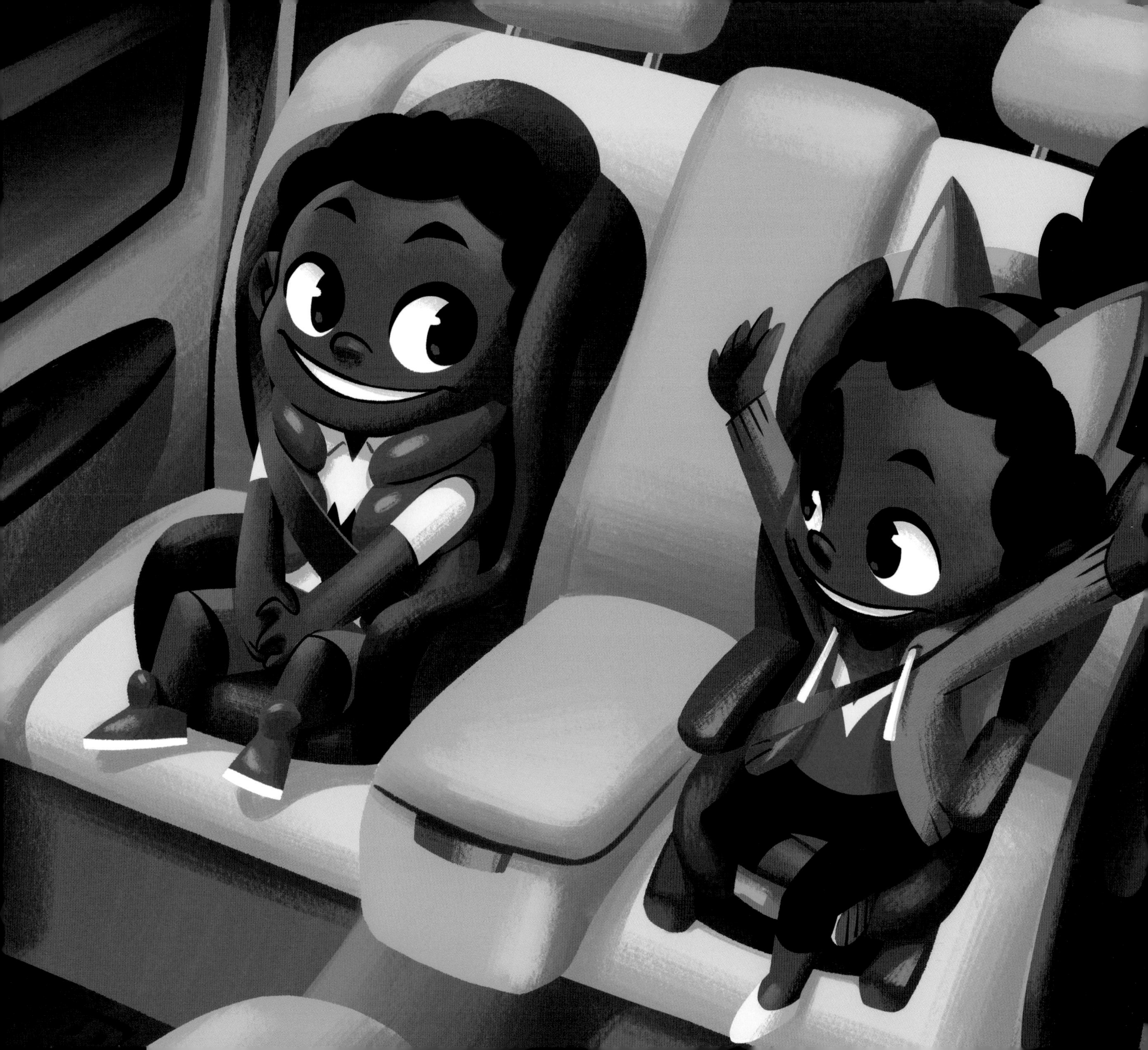

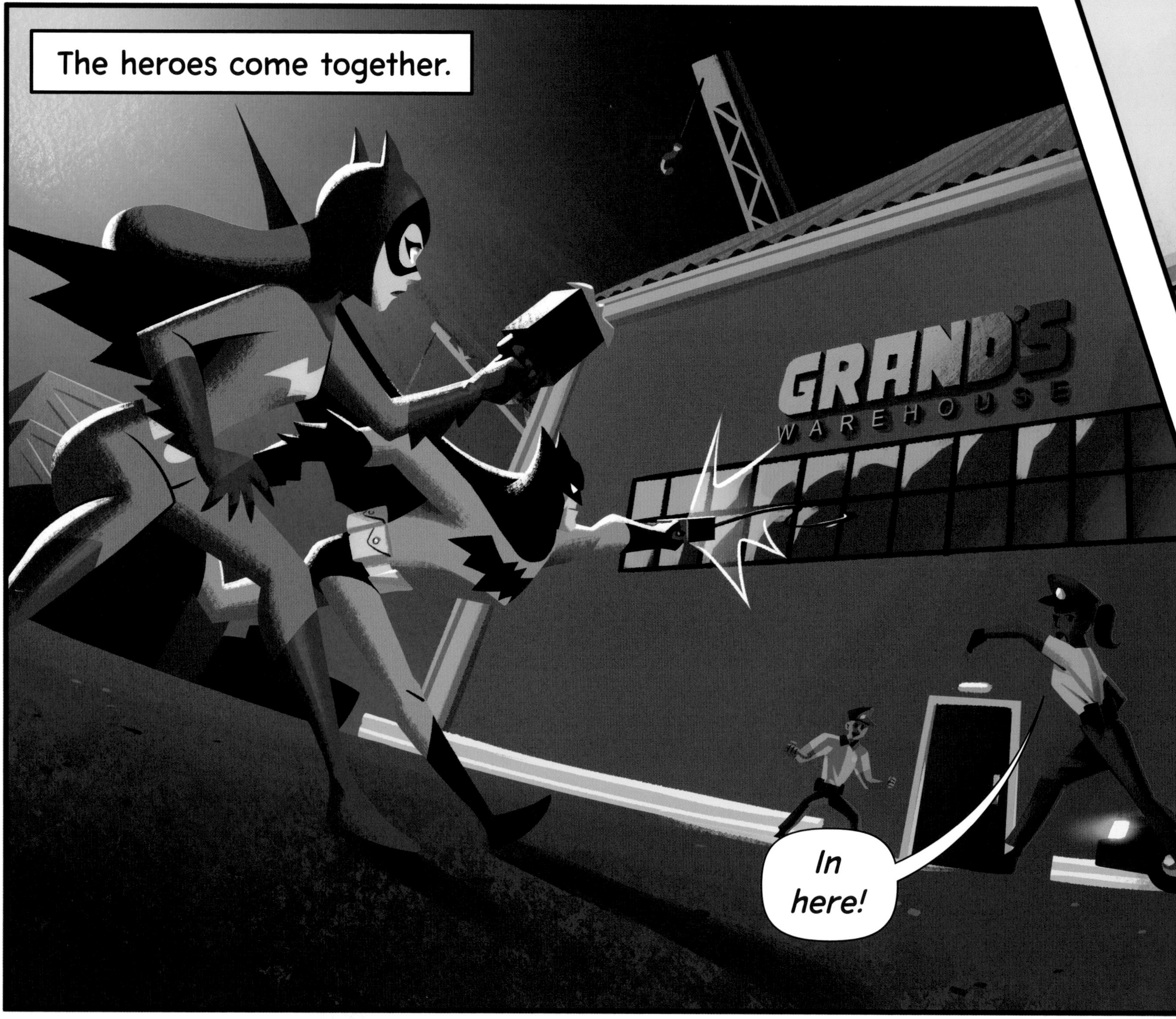
The heroes come together.
GRAND'S WAREHOUSE
In here!

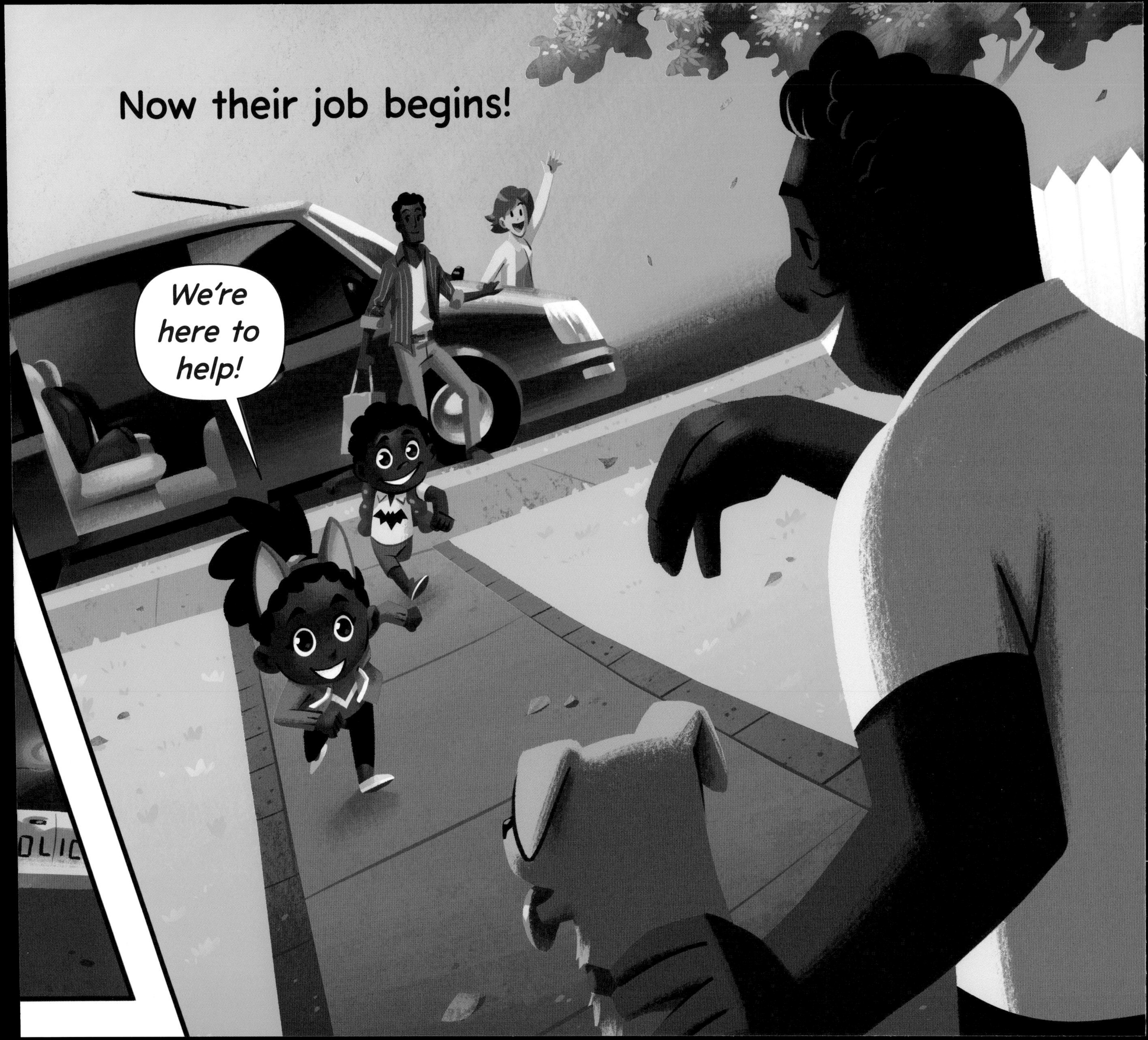
Now their job begins!
We're here to help!

More hands do more work.

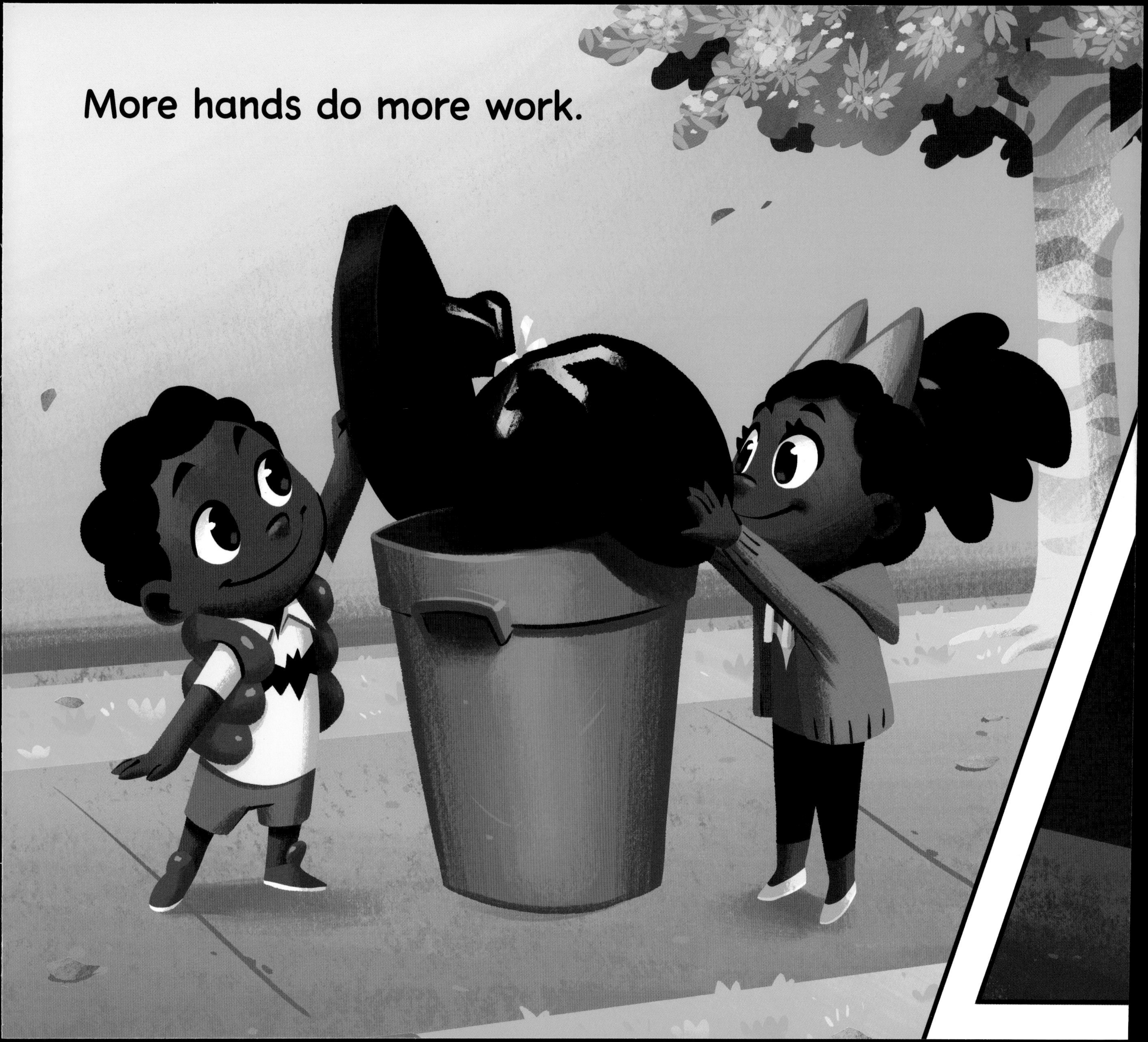

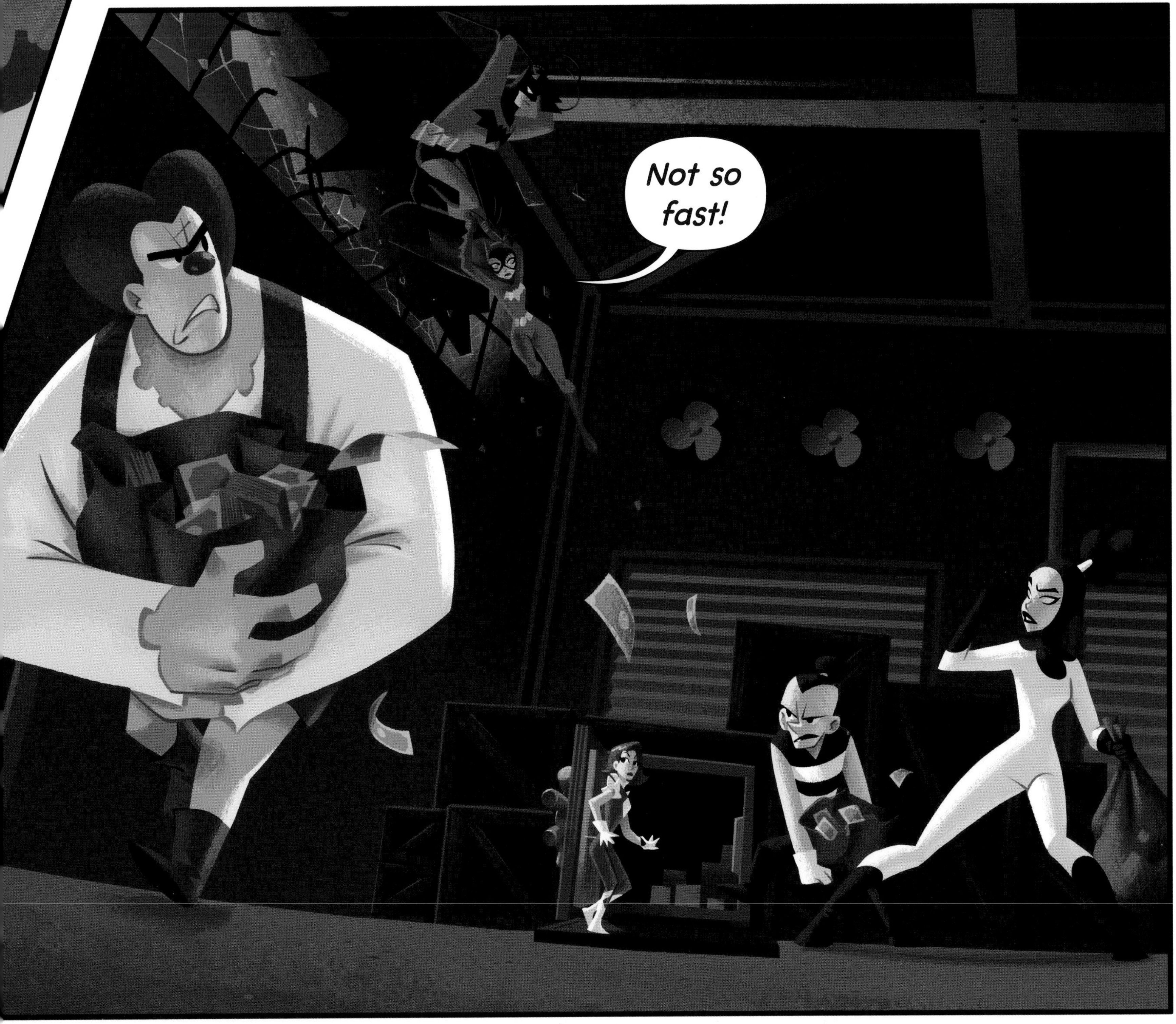
Not so fast!

Together, they
are stronger.

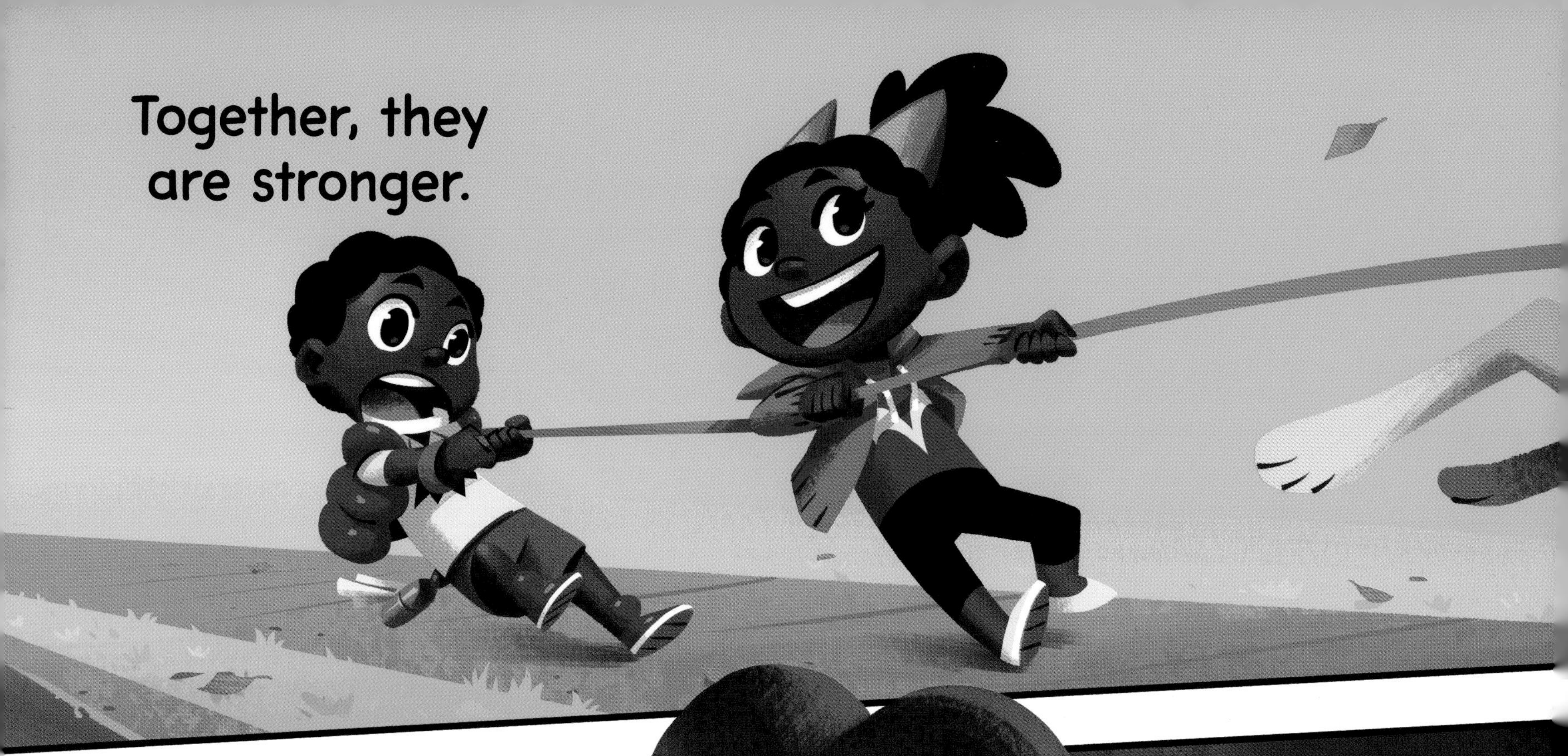

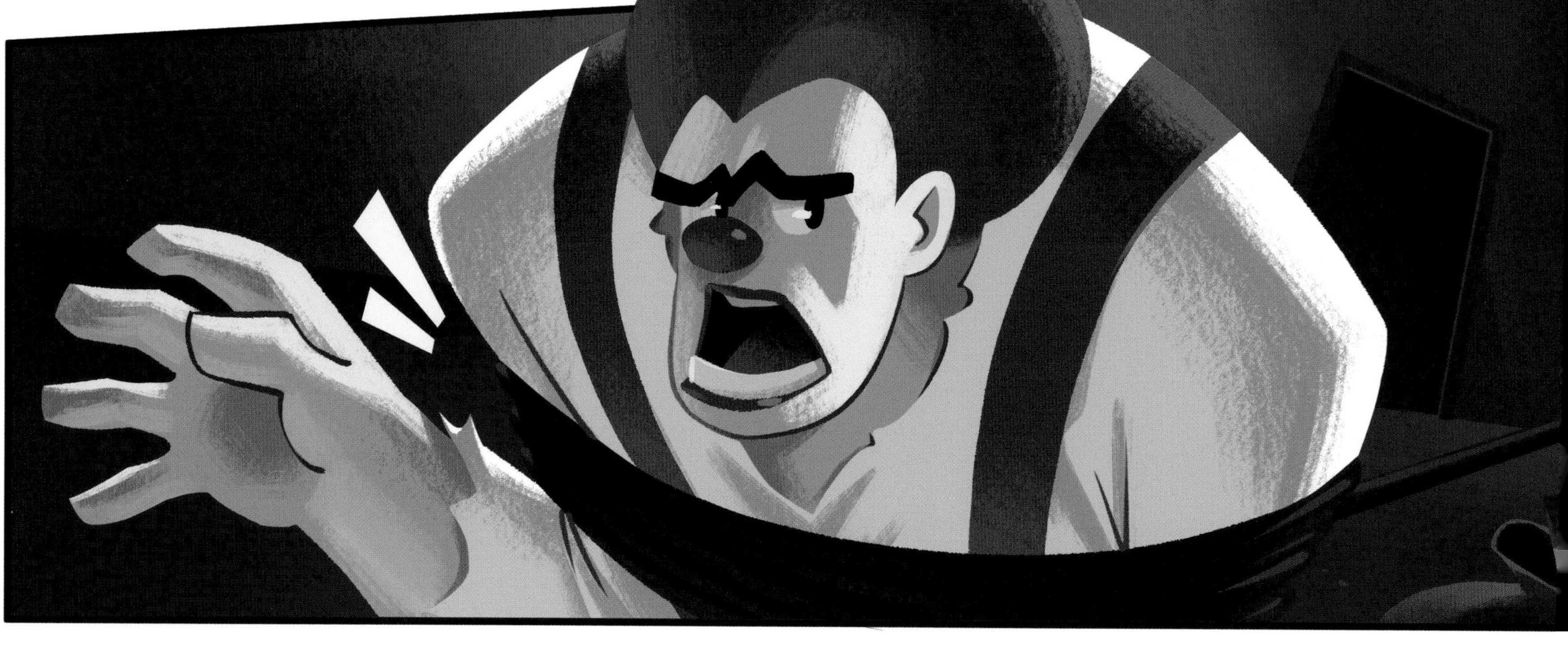

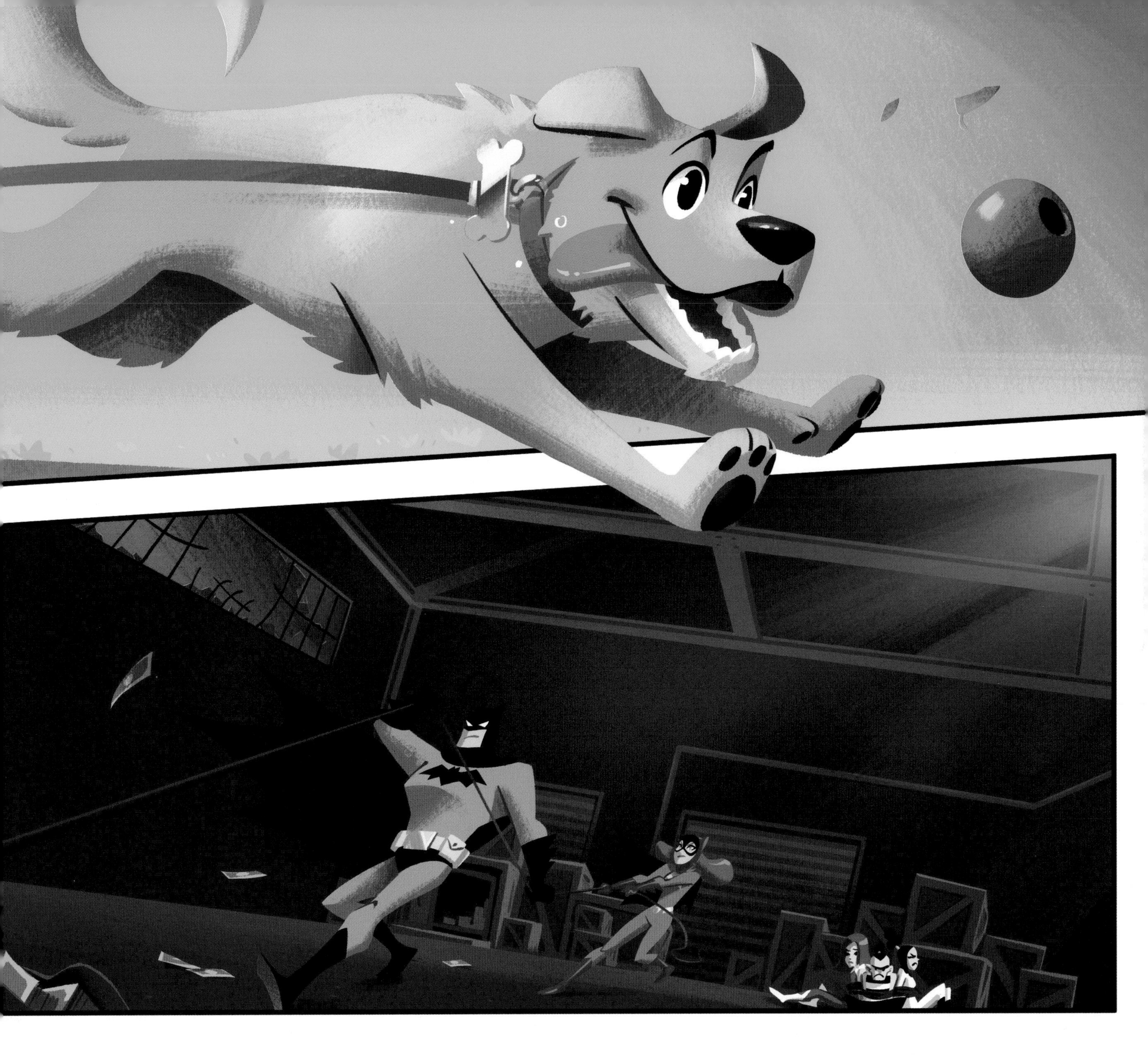

The job goes faster when they work side by side.

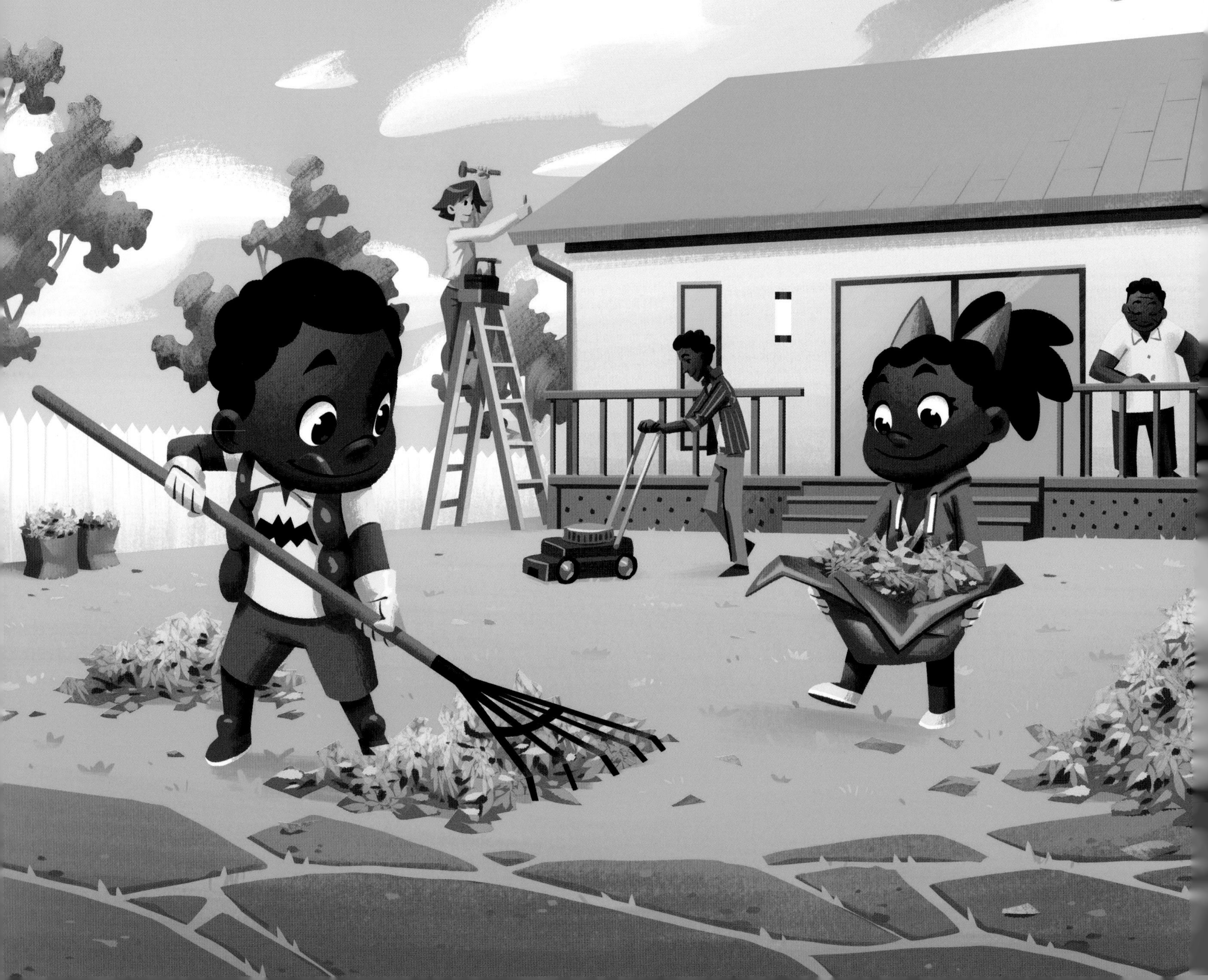

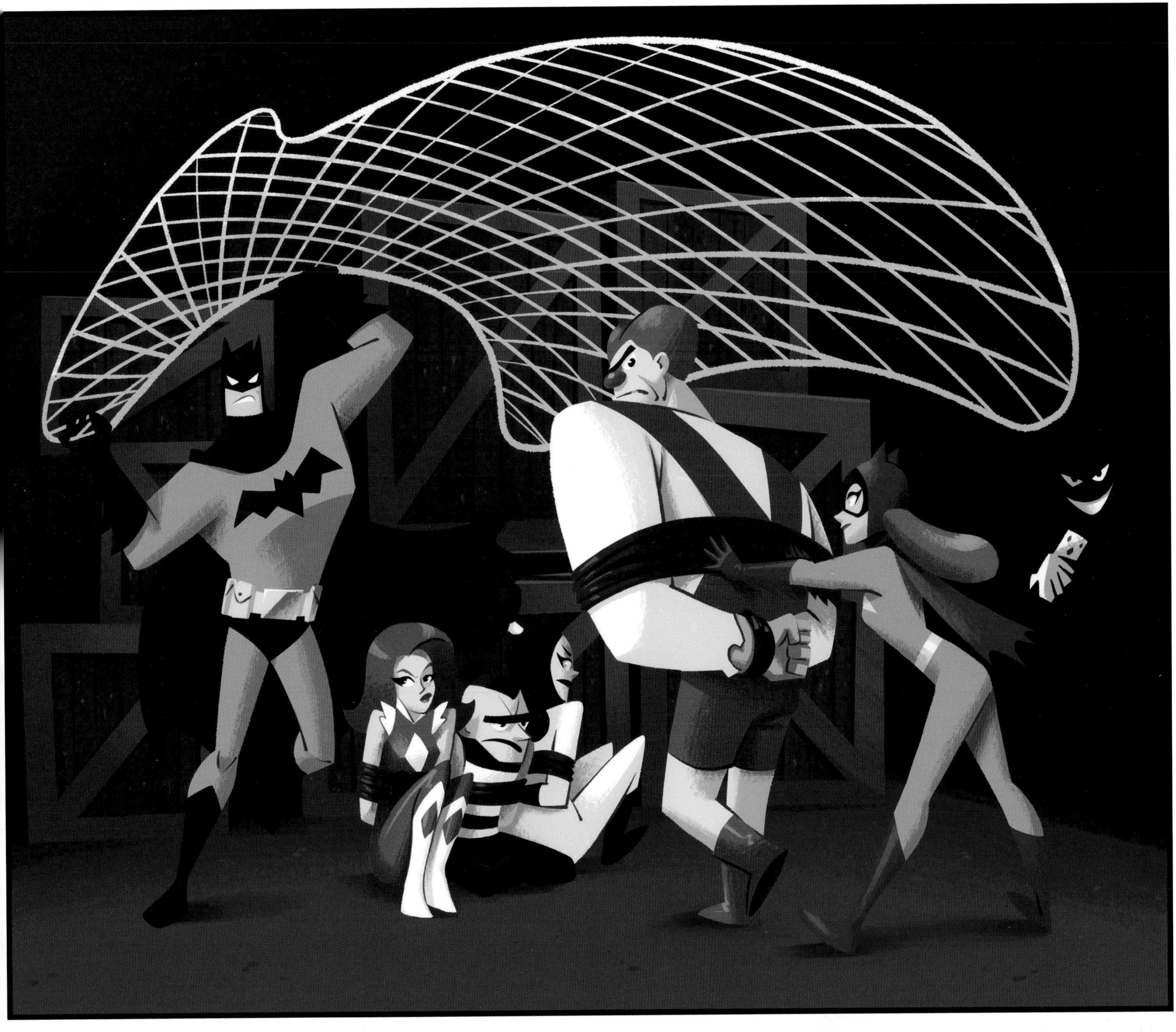

Together, they face the same challenges.

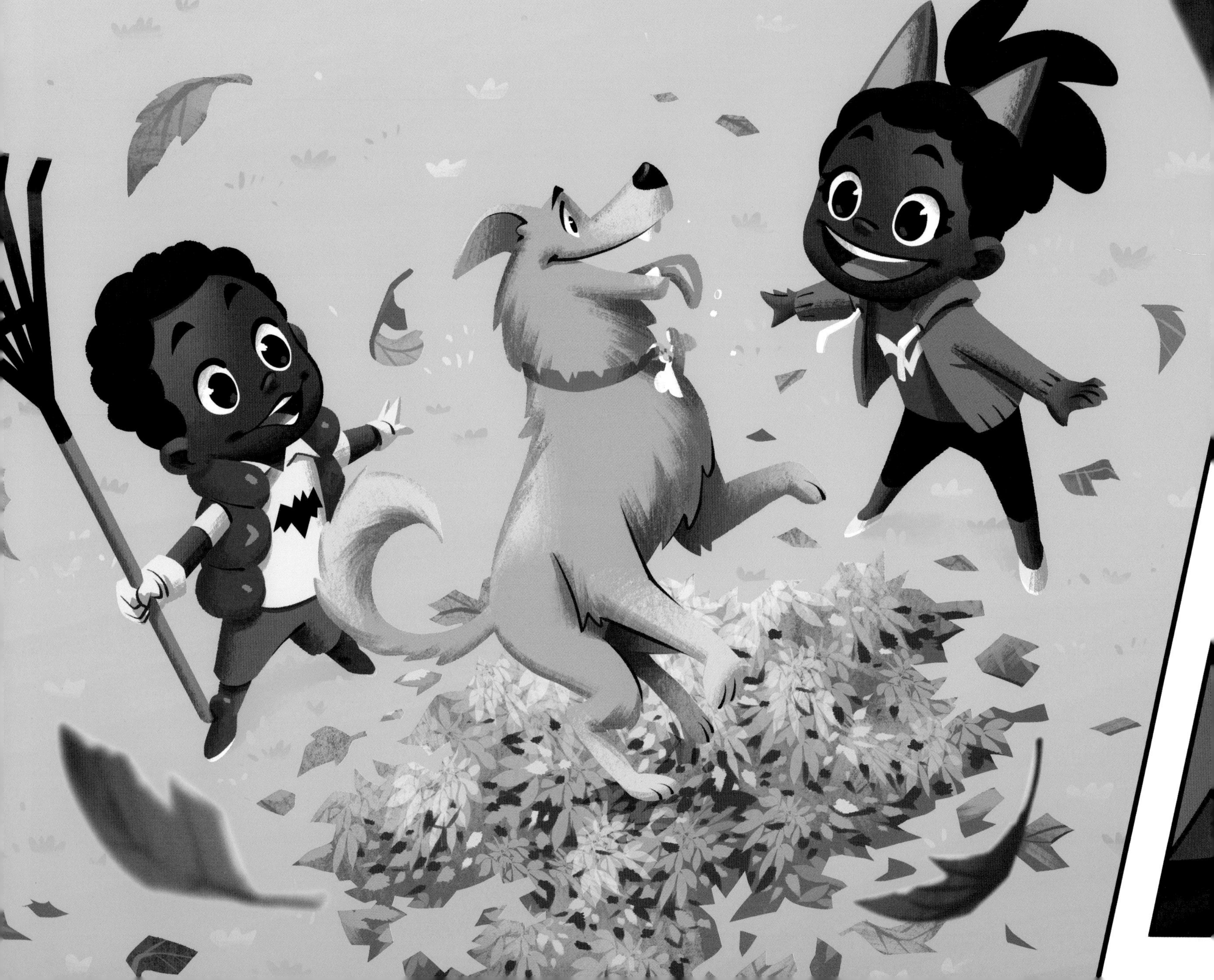

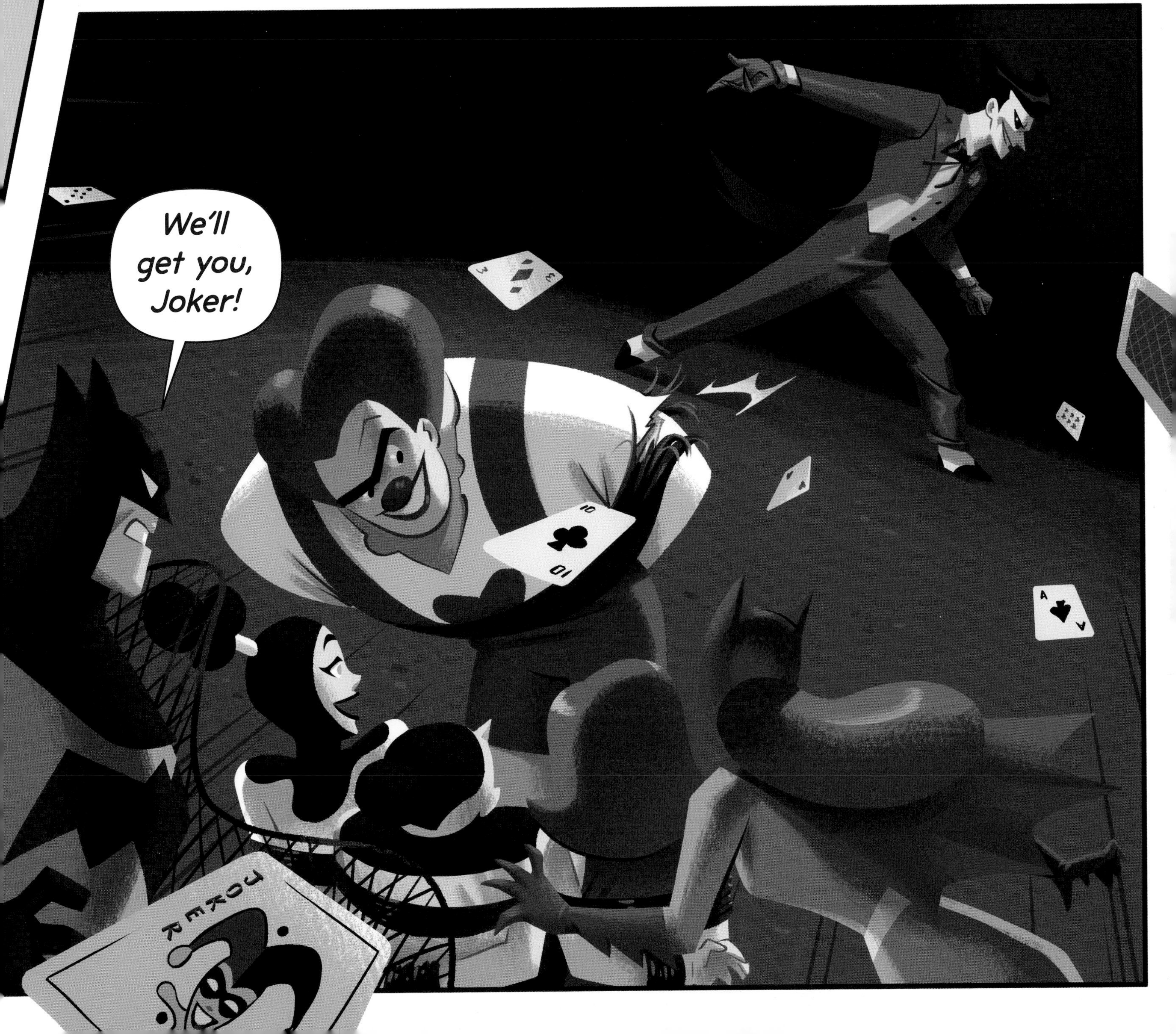
We'll get you, Joker!
JOKER

Both do their part . . .

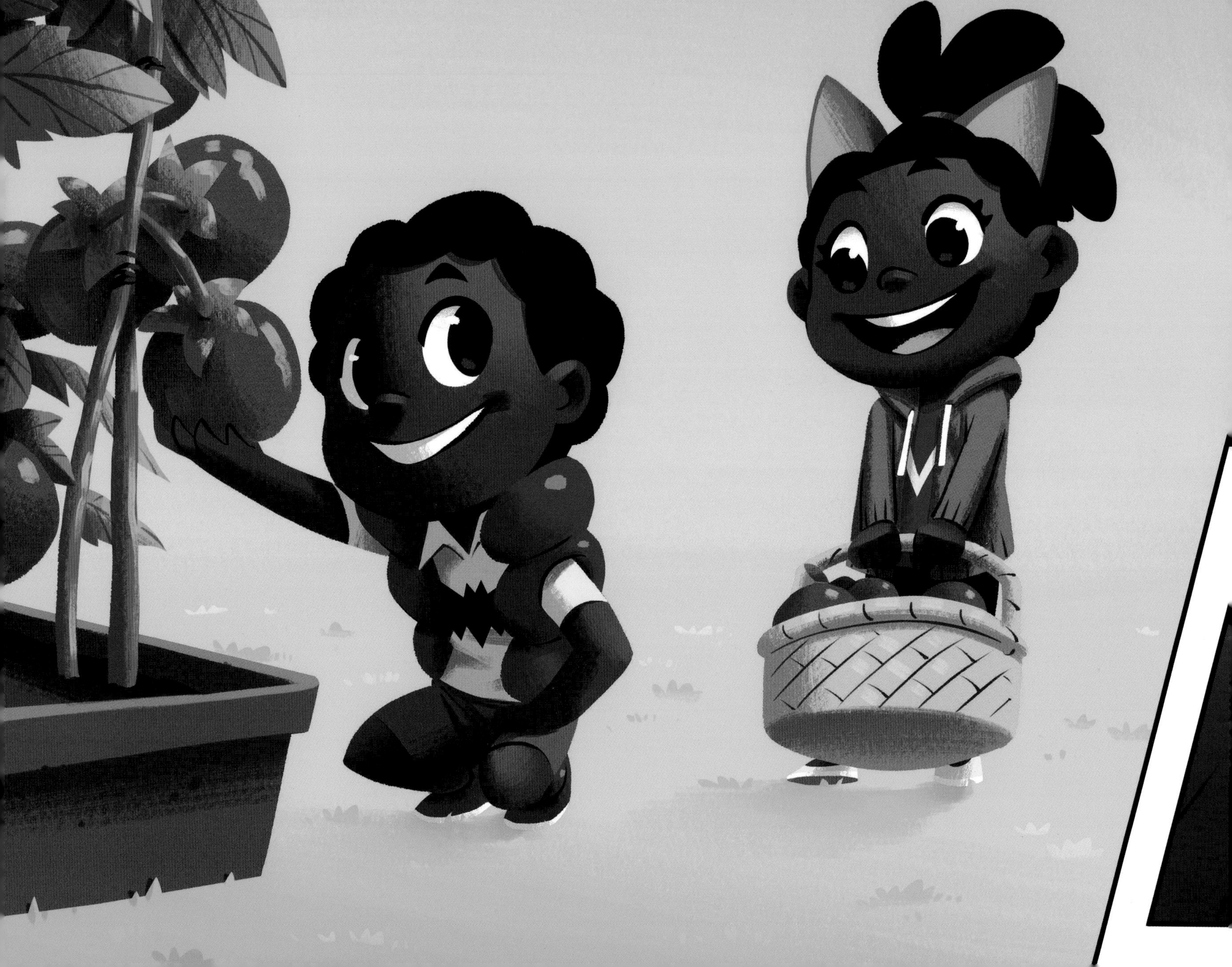

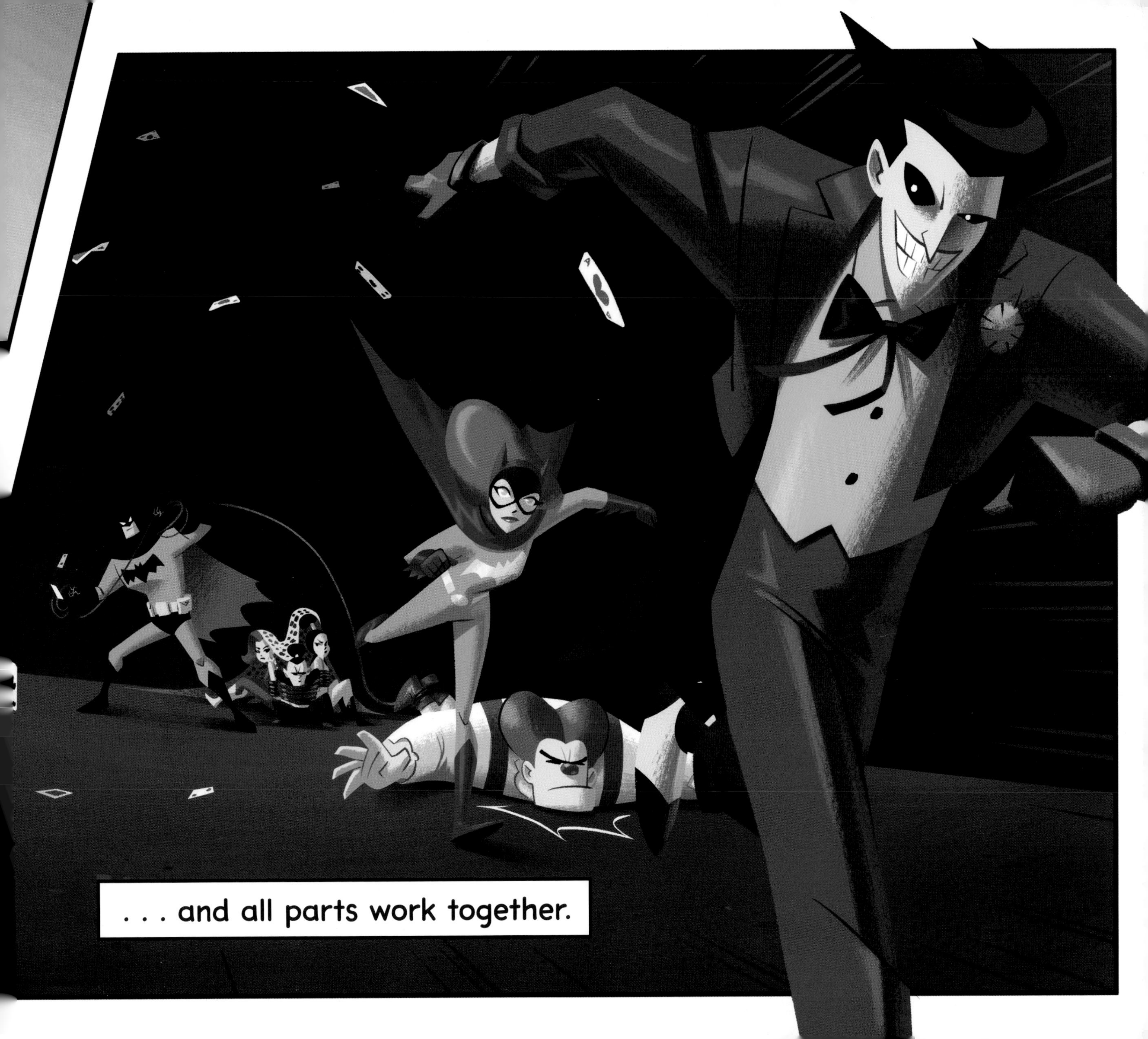
. . . and all parts work together.

Teamwork gives the boost . . .

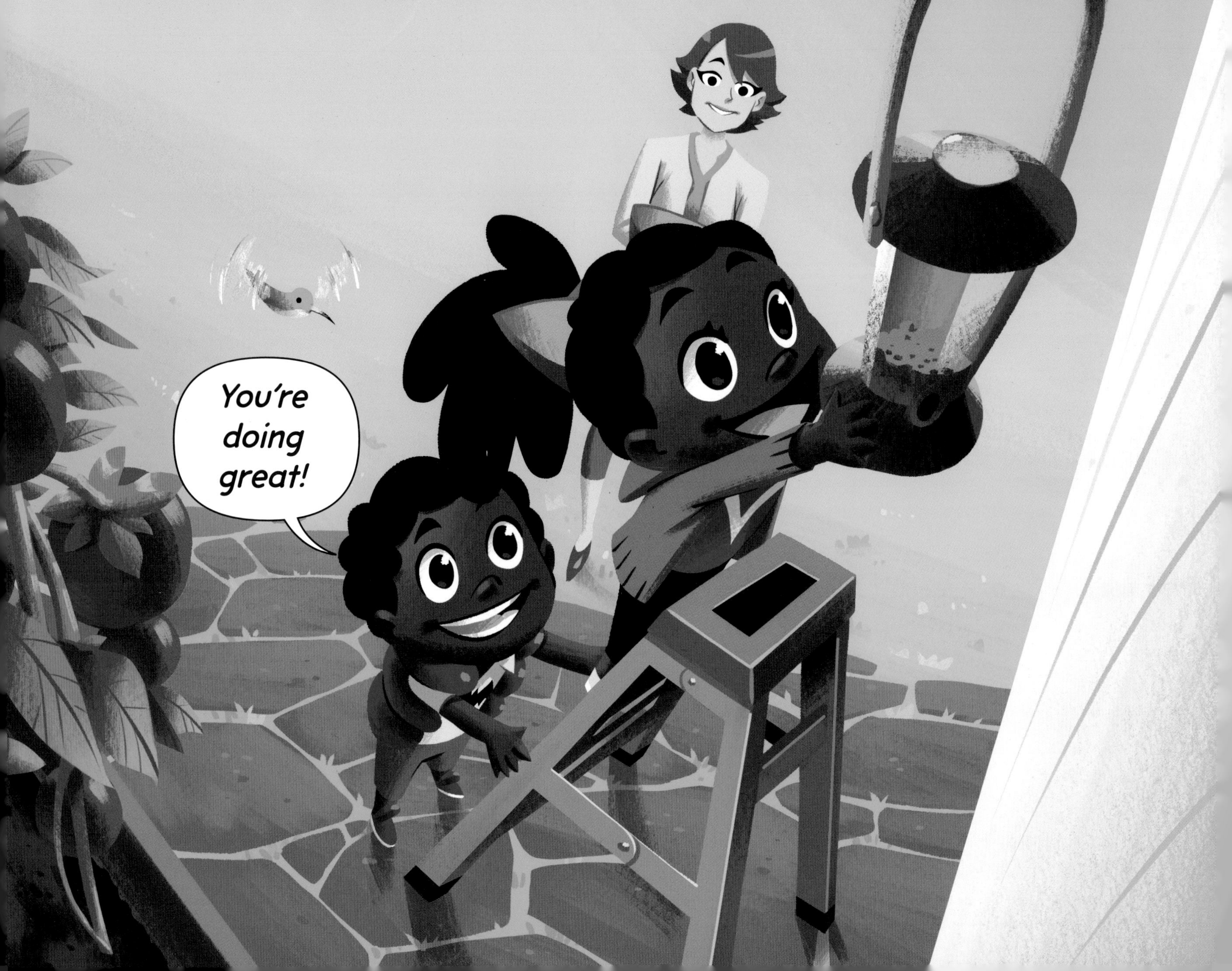
You're doing great!

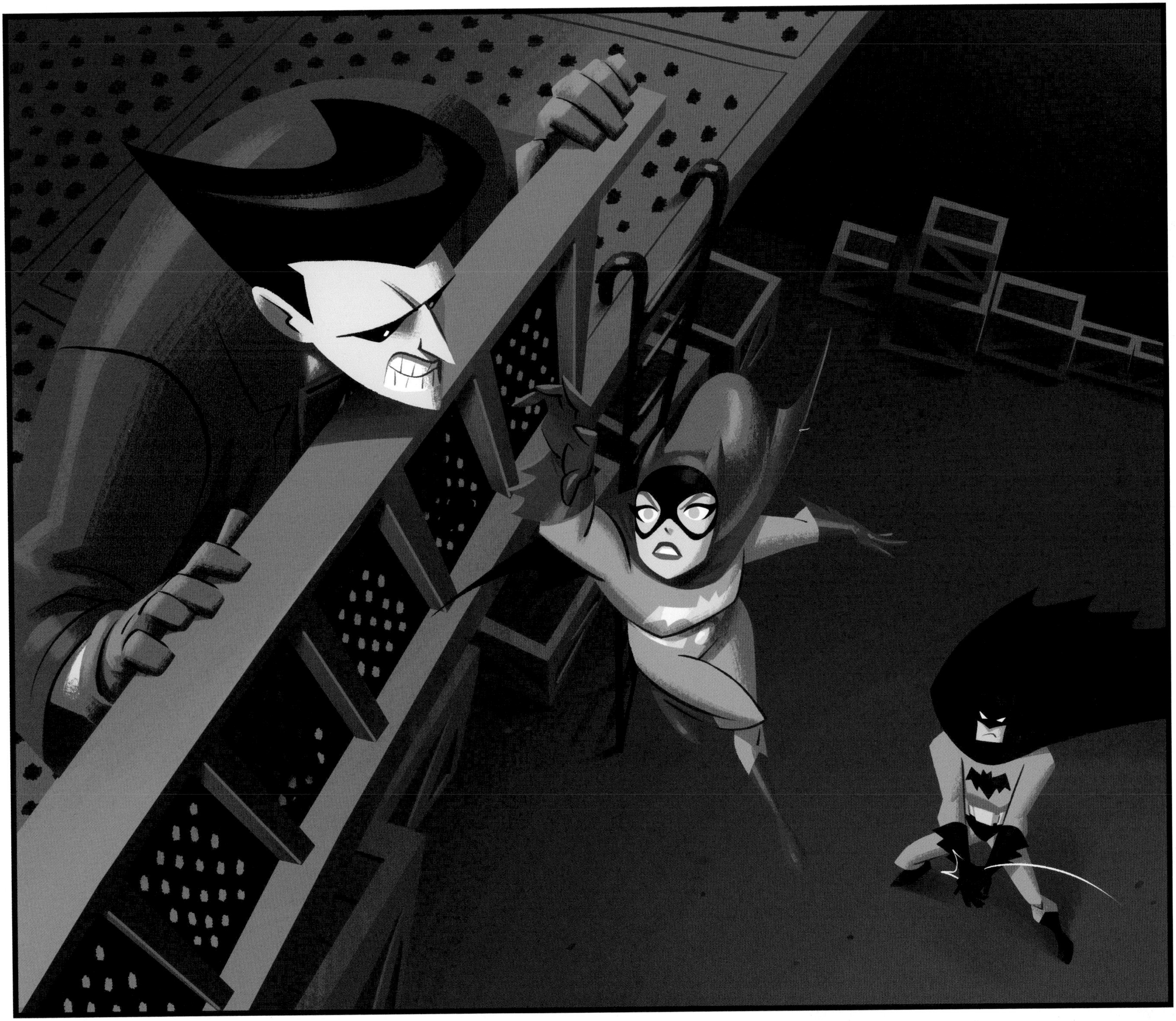

. . . to get the job done!

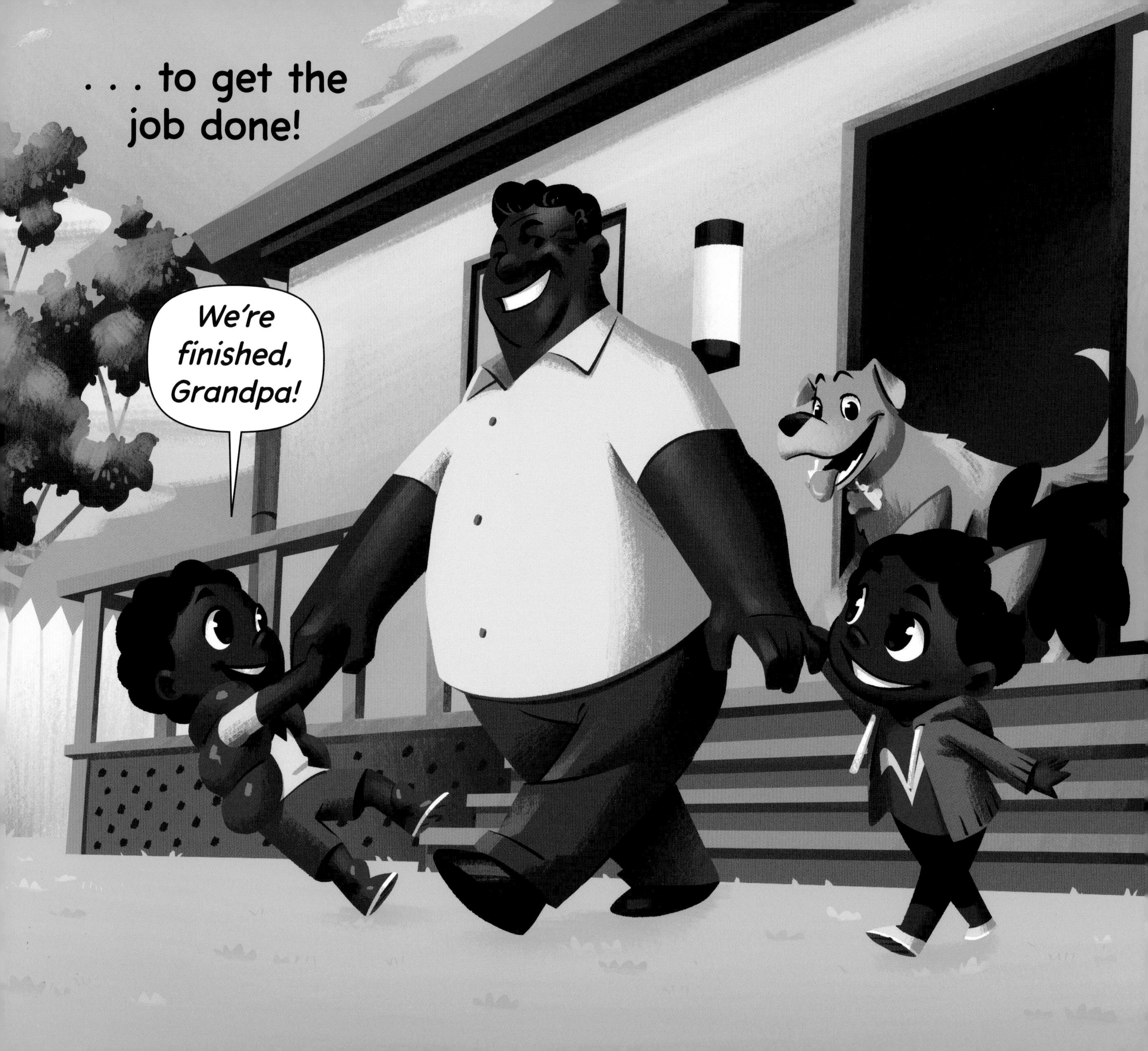
We're finished, Grandpa!

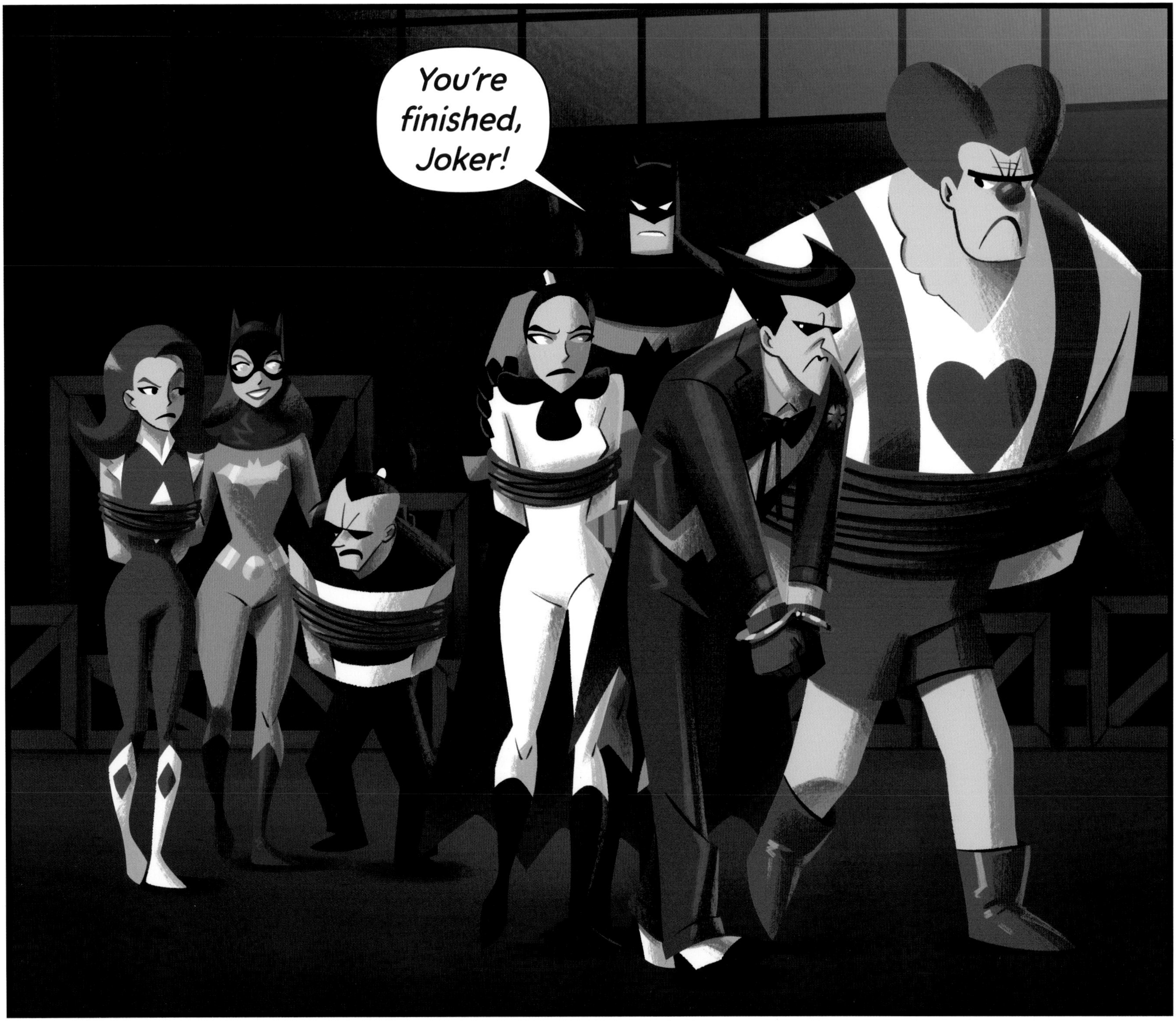
You're finished, Joker!

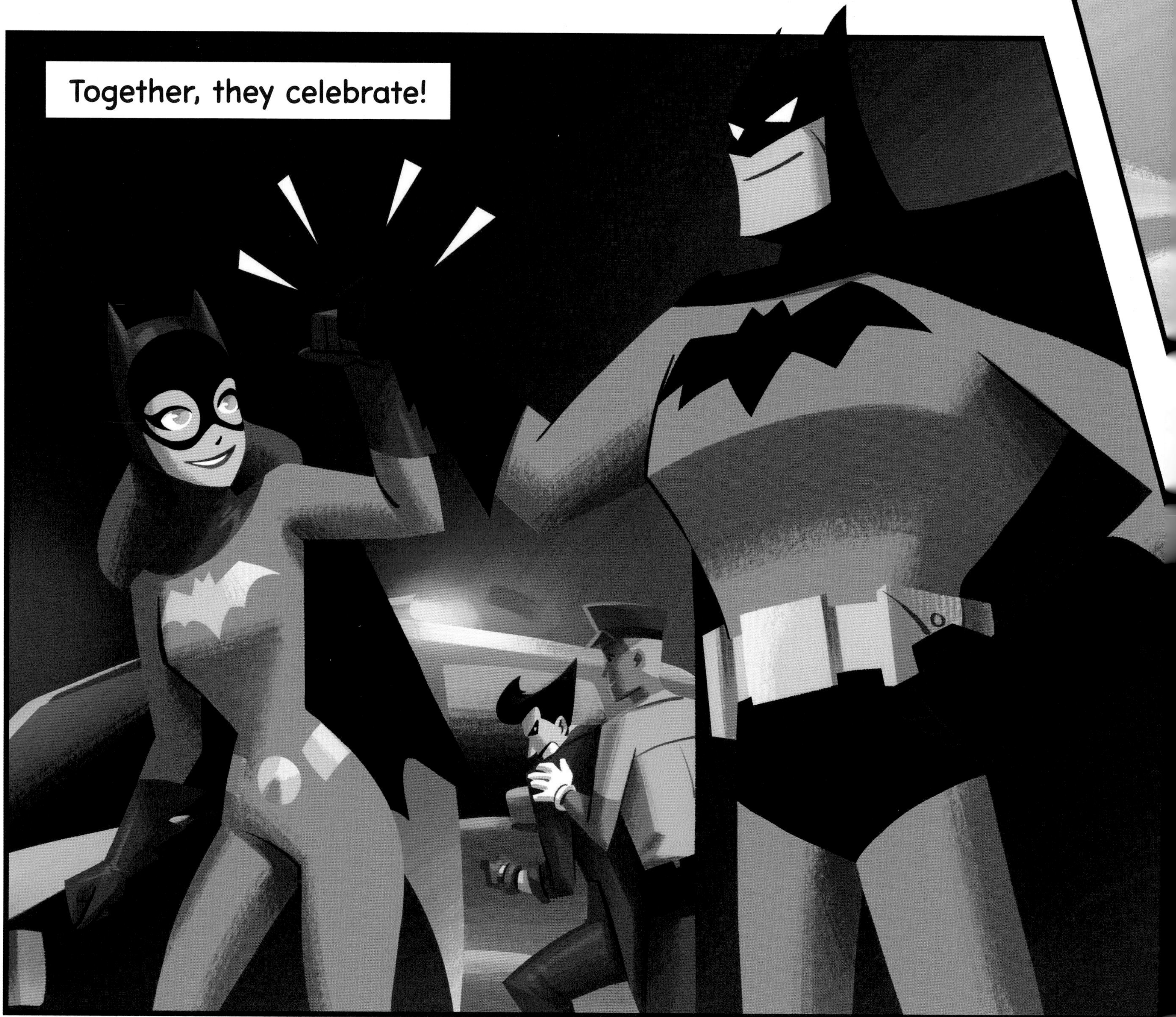
Together, they celebrate!

Sharing a victory adds to the fun.

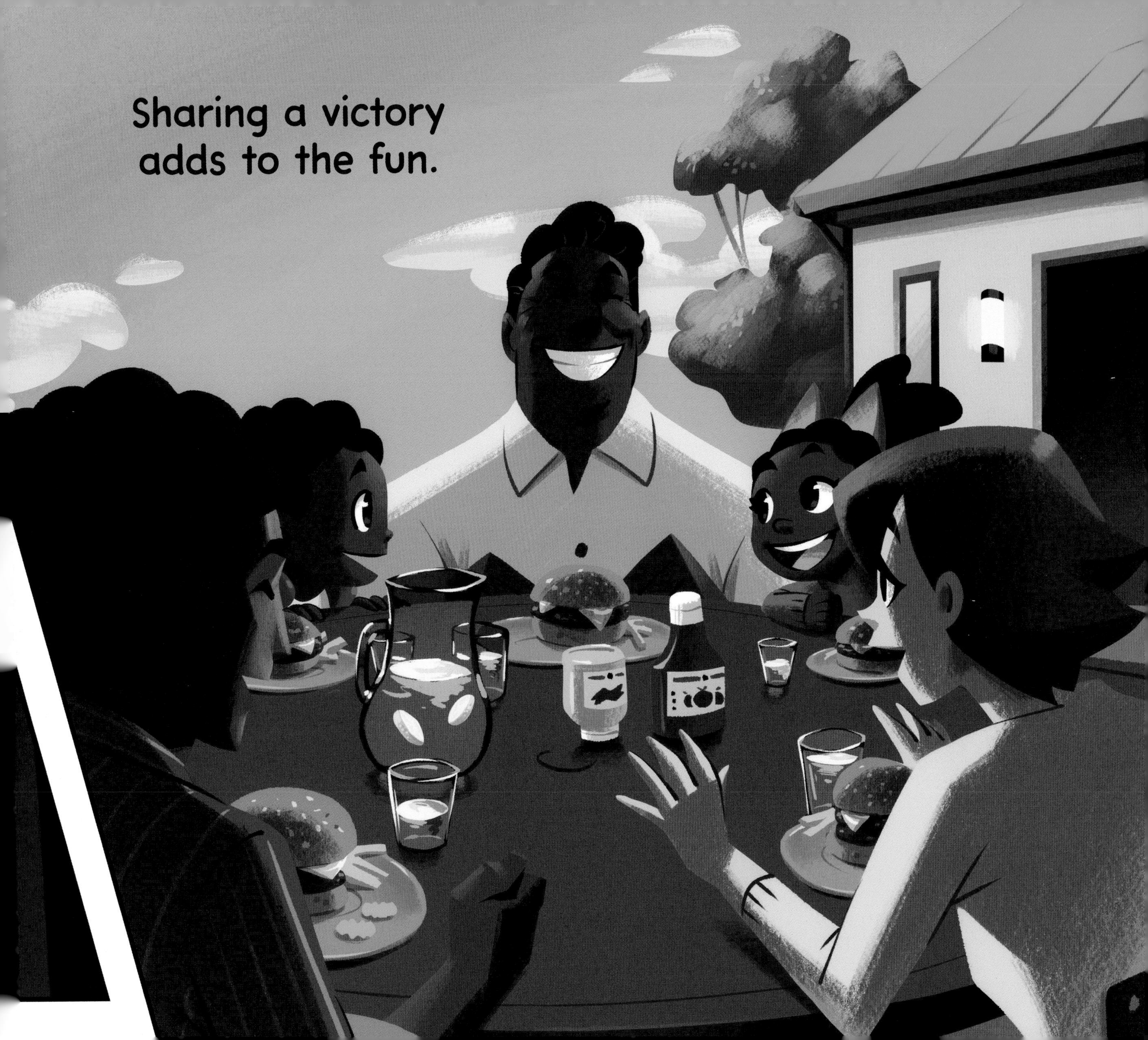

Great teamwork, heroes!

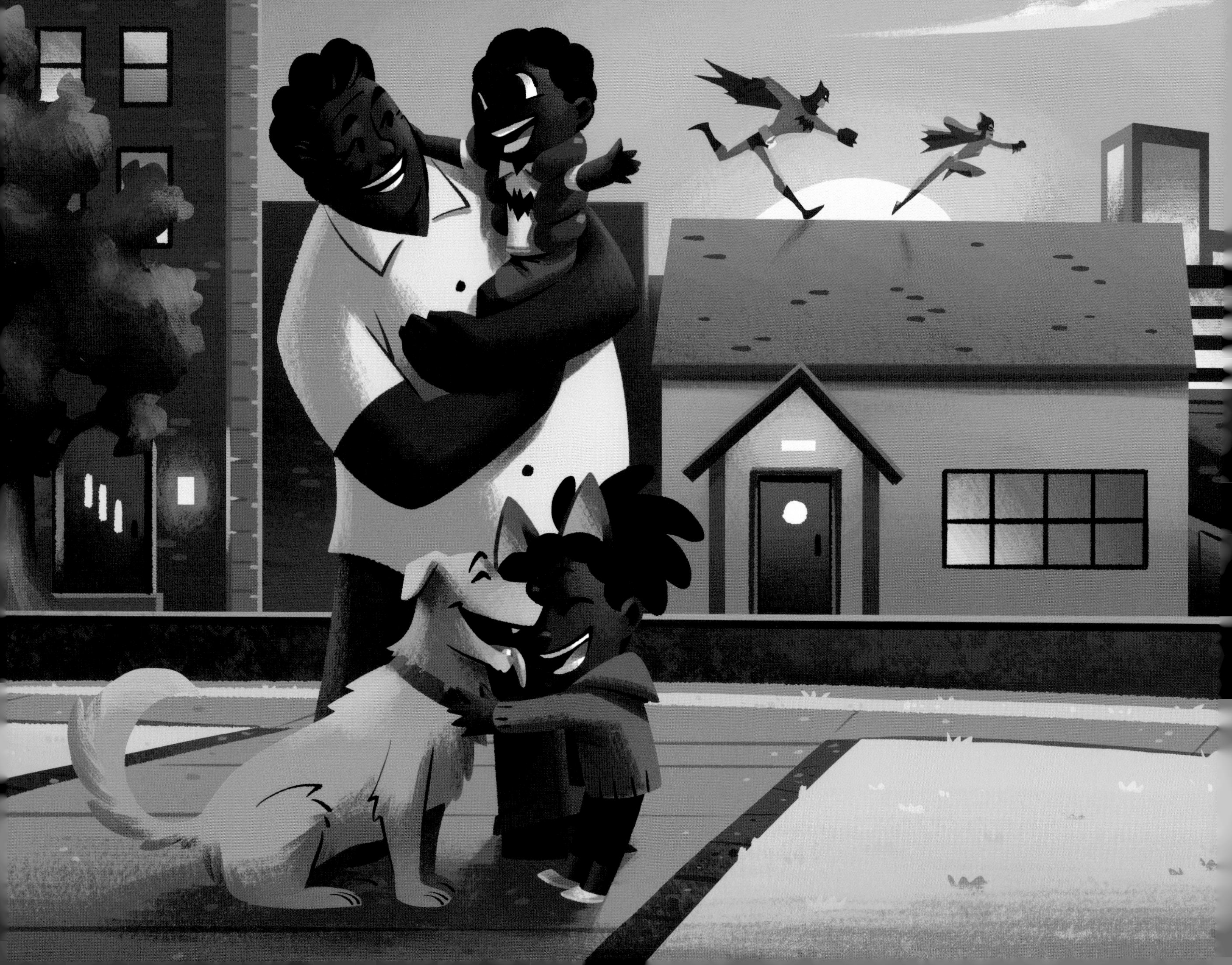

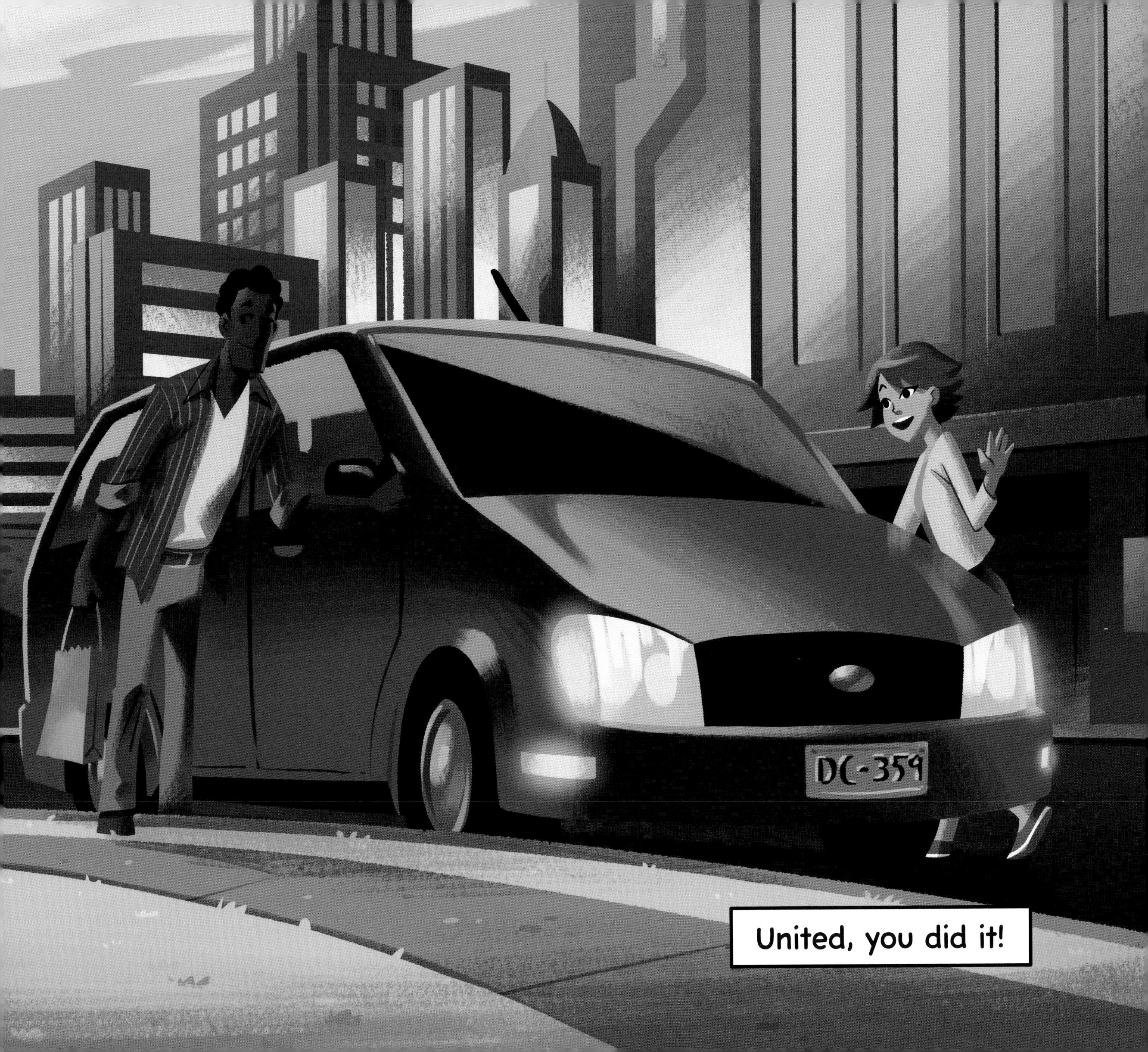
DC-359
United, you did it!

TALK TIME

Find a comfy spot and someone to talk to. It can be a parent, sibling, grandparent—anyone who you like to talk to. The theme of your talk is teamwork.

- Who do you like to work together with?
- What makes that person a good teammate?
- What makes working together better than working alone?

DRAW TIME

It's time to get creative! Grab some crayons or markers and a piece of paper. Now draw you and a friend as teamwork super heroes.

- What are your super hero names?
- What do your costumes look like?
- What teamwork superpowers do you and your friend have?
- Who are you and your friend helping with your superpowers?

PLAY TIME

It's always fun to play games with friends. Ask a few friends to play with you. Maybe invite a new friend to join!

THE PARACHUTE GAME

Gather some friends, a large bed sheet, and a beach ball. Lay the sheet flat on the ground and place the ball in the center. Now gather around the sheet and have each friend grab an edge. Work together to lift and lower the sheet to see how high you can launch the ball in the air.

THE HULA HOOP GAME

Ask your friends to stand in a circle. Now place a hula hoop over one friend's arm and ask everyone to join hands. Working together, find a way to move the hula hoop all the way around the circle without letting go of each other's hands!

UNITE TO BE A GREAT TEAM!

Work Together

Give Support

Take Turns

Don't Give Up

Be Encouraging

Celebrate Together